MODERN

Glamour. Power. Passion.

MILLS & BOON

First Published 2026
First Australian Paperback Edition 2026
ISBN 978 1 038 97448 8

MIX
Paper | Supporting responsible forestry
FSC® C001695

Published by
Harlequin Mills & Boon
An imprint of Harlequin Enterprises (Australia) Pty Limited (ABN 47 001 180 918), a subsidiary of HarperCollins Publishers Australia Pty Limited (ABN 36 009 913 517)
Level 19, 201 Elizabeth Street
SYDNEY NSW 2000 AUSTRALIA

Printed and bound in Australia by McPherson's Printing Group

Greek's Ring Of Redemption

Clare Connelly

MILLS & BOON

Books by Clare Connelly

Harlequin Modern

Pregnant Before the Proposal
Unwanted Royal Wife
Billion-Dollar Secret Between Them
Blackmail to White Veil

The Diamond Club

His Runaway Royal

Royally Tempted

Twins for His Majesty

A Greek Inheritance Game

Billion-Dollar Dating Deception
Tycoon's Terms of Engagement

Visit the Author Profile page
at millsandboon.com.au for more titles.

Clare Connelly was raised in small-town Australia among a family of avid readers. She spent much of her childhood up a tree, Harlequin book in hand. Clare is married to her own real-life hero, and they live in a bungalow near the sea with their two children. She is frequently found staring into space—a surefire sign she is in the world of her characters. She has a penchant for French food and ice-cold champagne, and Harlequin novels continue to be her favorite-ever books. Writing for Harlequin Presents is a long-held dream. Clare can be contacted via clareconnelly.com or on her Facebook page.

This book is a testament to The Love Shack crew: Annie West, Amy Andrews, Michelle Douglas, Jennifer St George and Ally Blake. You are incredible romance writers, wonderful women, supportive cheerleaders and friends. Thank you for the brainstorming, fun, memories and camaraderie. Nikos and Genevieve were born from our writers retreat, and I'm so grateful you helped me give them life.

PROLOGUE

EVEN AT THE best of times, the island of Therasia Notia, deep in the Aegean Sea, covered in ancient, now-dormant volcanic mountains, was rugged and impenetrable. But when the wind howled and the heavens opened up with lashing rain, and the sky split itself asunder with shocks of light, Nikos Konstantinou could almost convince himself he was the only man remaining on earth.

Just as he liked it.

Just as he knew he deserved to be.

Alone, isolated, and left to suffer, for the sins of his past. Sins for which there was no hope of repenting—no hope of repairing. The mother he hadn't been able to help, who'd turned to prostitution to keep a roof over their heads until she'd died, young and miserable. The wife he'd all but abandoned in his pursuit of success.

The life he'd once forged, through sheer grit, building his private equity business to the point of global domination, was now a distant memory. Though he kept himself apprised of operations, he was no longer hands-on in the way he'd once been—the satisfaction he'd drawn from those long, difficult days was now a poisoned chalice: something he was determined to deny himself. As penance, for what his ambition had done. The pain he'd caused.

He stood in the doorway to the small cabin he'd built, stone by stone, three years earlier, when he'd bought this island and come to it, not caring if he lived or died. Long, laborious days, finding rocks, carrying them up the steep hill, mortaring them into place until, eventually, walls began to take shape.

It had been a long time since Nikos had needed to work with his hands. Wealth had made him lazy, had risked turning him soft. Not that anyone who encountered him in the business world would ever have dreamt of describing him thus. No, Nikos was famed, not only for his competence, but also his ruthless determination.

It was that same determination that had seen him work twenty-hour days, losing himself to the empire he was intent on creating, at the expense of all else.

Even his marriage.

And his wife's happiness.

At the time, it had seemed like a necessary focus. Not only had he known extreme poverty as a boy, he'd also experienced the galling frustration of being told that ambition was pointless—to give up on wanting more. His father had likely been trying to adjust Nikos's goals to something more 'reasonable', but instead, he'd hammered the point into Nikos so hard that, with each scathing comment, Nikos's determination had formed like steel.

He closed his eyes and took a step further, so the rain now lashed him, his thick, dark hair loose almost to his bare shoulders, the denim shorts he wore covering his body only between the hips and mid-thigh. He spread his arms wide, and surrendered himself to the heavens, the gods, that were said to have created this mountainous island as a prison for one of their erstwhile demi-gods. If they wanted him, they could take him.

For Nikos Konstantinou, one of the most successful billionaires in the entire world, had nothing and no one to live for, and every day, he wondered if it might be his last. His wife had died miserable, because of his neglect; surely he didn't deserve anything other than the same fate?

CHAPTER ONE

GENEVIEVE WILSON COULDN'T claim that setting sail on her own across the Aegean was her stupidest mistake ever—clearly that honour rested on the day she'd said 'yes' to marrying her sadistic bastard of an ex-husband—but it was definitely in the top three.

After all, she hadn't sailed since she was a child. Though she'd sailed then often, and had been very good at it, it turned out sailing was nothing like riding a bike. Some parts were muscle memory, of course. Others common sense. And if the waters had stayed calm, as they'd been when she set off, then most likely she would have been okay—if a little shaken by the experience.

But the storm that whipped up almost out of nowhere, turning the placid Aegean into a turbulent, washing-machine-like high tide, quickly began to rock her small craft from side to side in a way that was instantly terrifying. The rain made it almost impossible to see, and her hands kept slipping on the ropes. Every lesson her father had taught Genevieve, as a girl, seemed to wash out to sea.

Helplessness gripped her. Helplessness and misery. Would anyone even care if the boat capsized and she was lost to the depths of the ocean? Not her now ex-husband. There was no one else. Her father had died when she was little more than a girl, her mother a few years ago, after a series of strokes that had seen her hospitalised for more than a year, before she passed away in her sleep one night. Any friends she'd once been close to had fallen by the wayside as Genevieve had turned herself inside out to become the perfect political wife her senator husband had required, not even missing a step after her mother's death, when her world had been knocked completely off course. Who was there to miss or mourn her?

The frigid and brutal reality of that was, if anything, a talisman to Genevieve. She'd been through too much to give up now. Finally, she had her freedom. At least, in a sense. Courtesy of her mother's eye-watering hospital bills, she was too financially indebted to her ex, who was paying off the instalments, to know exactly how to explore her freedom. At least she was no longer under his complete control—no longer the perfect, submissive trophy wife to be used and humiliated by him depending on his whims and needs. She was setting out on the second phase of her life, a time of rebuilding. She wouldn't die friendless and alone here, where no one would even think to look for her.

There was nothing for it. She needed to bring the boat to shore somewhere. A port in the storm, literally. She cast about, her eyes squinting against the hard-falling rain, until finally, a lightning bolt seemed to burst almost directly overhead, making her scream at the same time she recognised something silhouetted against the storm-darkened sky.

A mountain. And mountains in the middle of the ocean could mean only one thing: an island.

Tacking the boat to the south, she prayed that she could

make it there, even as she continued to be rocked violently from side to side, so it was almost impossible to hold her course, let alone stay on board. Enormous waves crashed over the sides, dousing her, and then, finally, she was close enough to shore to jump from the boat. She leaped over the rail, and just in time! As she watched, and tried to work out how to get the boat aground enough to shore, it rocked high on a wave and then capsized, the sail snapping against the seafloor, so she cried out and pressed her hands to her mouth.

It wasn't her most pressing concern, but in the back of her mind she hated to think how much it was going to cost her in damages to the hire company. She had no idea if the insurance policy she'd taken out would cover this sort of act of stupidity. What kind of person rode a sailing boat right into a storm?

That was a bridge she would cross down the track. If she lived to make it that far. For now, she needed shelter. She looked around, helplessly, eyes chasing the rugged coastline of this mountain. She'd become disorientated some time ago, and the map she'd taken from her small, mid-century hotel's lobby, showing the Greek islands, had blown out to sea long ago. She had no idea which island she'd landed on, but she had a sinking suspicion that it might be one of those tiny, uninhabited ones. Which did not bode well for a woman who now had no phone, no handbag and no boat.

She couldn't panic, though.

It had taken grit and determination to extricate herself from her marriage; these were skills she now knew she had in abundance.

Genevieve began to walk. She was so wet that her

shorts and long-sleeved shirt were plastered to her body, and her shoes squelched as she moved away from the shallows and began to look around once more. She was in a cove, and there was no sign of habitation. But that didn't mean the whole place was deserted.

Ignoring the dark fears in her mind, that she was indeed stranded on the unluckiest island in the entire Aegean, she began to traipse along the sand, figuring she could start tracking a perimeter, looking for both signs of life and some kind of shelter. Whichever came first. Dark clouds were rolling over the island, which, combined with the pouring rain, made it impossible to see too far in front of her.

It took a monumental effort to hold onto hope, but more than an hour after crashing onto this island, while the storm continued to rage and her body was exhausted and covered in goosebumps, she finally saw something to give her hope. Even just the tiniest flicker of it. The storm felt like a metaphor for her whole freaking life. One thing after the other, and just when she was at her lowest ebb, bam. Something worse.

Some way in the distance, high up on a hill, was a light. Warm and golden, and not a trick conjured by her desperation. She changed direction immediately, picking her way across the sand and onto the grass behind it. Dense forest followed, which flooded her with terror. Because here, she heard animal noises, and she couldn't help but imagine she'd gone from the frying pan and into the fire. She might have escaped death at sea, but between herself and the golden light stood miles of forest, and it was not implausible to imagine being mauled by whatever animal was making that persistent call.

With the same determination she'd employed in her marriage, to ignore her husband's affairs and the cold brutality with which he treated her, she went on, one step after the other. There was no path to follow, and she slipped, many times, cutting her leg and badly hurting her arm, but eventually she came to a clearing and saw, to her immense and all-consuming relief, that the golden glow was indeed a dwelling. A house! Well, a house of sorts. Four walls and a roof, and it clearly had electricity. She didn't stop to think about who might be inside, but rather rushed gratefully towards it and lifted a hand, banging on the door as though her life depended on it.

Which, come to think of it, it did.

Silence met her thumping. She kept knocking. And minutes later, with the rain still gushing over her and the sky lighting up every few minutes with blades of white, as thunder rolled right into her ear canal, she knew she had little choice but to push open the door. After all, the cabin could well be empty, the light left on by whoever had last occupied it.

Either way, she wasn't going to stay standing out here, getting more and more sodden by the minute, all but inviting lightning to fry her innards.

She pushed the door tentatively at first and then all the way, stepping in with a small grimace at how much water she was dripping onto the rustic timber floor. But there was a fire across the room, glowing warm and golden, so she knew two things immediately: firstly, she wasn't alone. Secondly, she was too cold to care.

Walking quickly across the room, she made it to the hearth and turned her back on it, still dropping huge amounts of water on the ground, as she let the heat wrap around her, comforting and reassuring. She'd been standing there only a moment when another door, on the other wall of the cabin, opened, and a man strode from what her brain quickly suggested must have been a bathroom. Why? Because he was as naked as the day he was born, and every bit as rugged as the forest she'd hiked through to make it to his cabin.

She could only stare as he stopped walking and stared right back. Stare at his height and breadth, at arms that were muscular and a broad, hair-roughened chest that was rippling with abdominal muscles, wide shoulders that almost seemed to suggest he could carry the weight of the world on them. His hips were narrow, compared to his broad chest, but his legs were as muscly and sinewy as his arms, all strength and formidable power in those limbs. He was tall—easily six and a half feet—and handsome in a raw, animalistic sort of way, with features that were chiselled and rough, symmetrical and completely pleasing. His eyes were a dark grey, like the stormy ocean that had tormented her hours earlier, and his hair wasn't cut fashionably short—it might have been, once upon a time, but now it caressed his neck, though it was wet and brushed back from his brow.

As for his very masculine anatomy, her cheeks flushed pink at the way he stood before her, glorious, uncaring, and huge all over.

The thunderous expression on his face should have given her cause for concern, but it was all so shocking and confronting, so confusing, that she could only stand there and drink in the sight of him.

'I—you're—' She tried to speak, to explain, but she was still shivering, and her mouth wouldn't cooperate.

Grimly, he walked towards her, the thunderclouds in his expression growing, if it was possible, even darker.

'We will deal with the pleasantries later. You look as though you are about to pass out. Are you?' His accent was unmistakably Greek, but his English was fluent.

'I—don't—' She closed her eyes then as, indeed, a wave of exhaustion and nausea hit her, combining with the icy chill in her veins. 'I'll be okay,' she said, but slowly, softly, the words lacking conviction.

He grunted and then, to Genevieve's absolute shock, he was lifting her up and cradling her against his naked chest, carrying her across the sparsely furnished cabin, towards the door he'd emerged from a moment earlier. It was almost as large as the other room, though it had only a shower, a basin and a toilet. He placed her down on the tiled floor of the shower and began to run the water. Then, to Genevieve's further shock, his hands curled around the fabric of her shirt and began to lift it.

'D-don't,' she stammered, feeling she must protest. It didn't occur to her to fear the man, despite the notable differences in their size and strength. He was rugged, yes, but there was nothing about him that screamed 'violent'. Her protestation then was all about modesty. Her ex-husband was the only man who'd seen her naked. It was strange to contemplate letting a stranger see all of her bared. And yet, it was also exhilarating. James, for one, would hate it—and that thought was infinitely appealing.

'You need to get out of these clothes.'

'I can manage,' she said, finally finding her voice, and hoping that she wasn't lying.

'Can you? Show me.'

'I'm not going to get undressed in front of you.'

'And I have no intention of leaving you here to pass out on your own. So?'

'I'm not going to—'

'We can argue later, as well,' he said, lips forming a grim line. 'All I care about, right now, is that you do not die on my watch. Whoever you are, and wherever you came from, is not my concern. What you do after leaving here is also of no interest. But for now, I intend that you stay alive. If not least because the inconvenience of having to report your death is the last thing I want.'

She was so shocked that she did reach for her shirt then, but before she lifted it off she turned her back on him so her breasts were shielded from his sight. Her shorts followed, but she kept her briefs on.

The water, in contrast to the rain outside, was scorching and with each moment she stood beneath it, she felt a little strength return. Though her legs felt like jelly after what must have been a ten-mile hike, most of it uphill and over uneven terrain. Fear had made her run much of the way.

He reached past her, his thick, strong arm brushing her side as he flicked off the water and then seconds later wrapped a large, coarse towel around her shoulders. 'Can you walk or do you need to be carried?'

There was no way she was going to admit even a hint of weakness to this man, even though her legs felt as though they were impossibly trembly. 'I can walk.'

'Show me.'

He crossed his arms over his chest, apparently uncaring that he was still naked.

'Do you own clothes?' she muttered, aware that she sounded like a petulant child.

In the living area once more, he lifted a chair towards the fireplace and set it down. 'Sit.'

'I'm not a puppy, you know. You can speak to me like a fellow human being. Or is courtesy in short supply out here, in the middle of nowhere?'

'I didn't ask you to come into my home, and if it weren't for the fact you could not survive out there—' he jerked his thumb towards the single window of this cabin, large and just to the right of the front door '—I would have no compunction in turfing you out. Perhaps once the storm passes...'

'Definitely once the storm passes,' she responded, though she did sit on the chair, careful to keep the towel wrapped around herself, protecting her modesty.

'Good.' He turned away then, disappearing to a rustic-looking piece of furniture near the large bed, and removing—to her relief—a pair of cotton boxer briefs. He dragged them up his body but Genevieve was startled to discover that, clothes or no clothes, the sight of him in all his glorious nudity was burned into her brain.

She looked away quickly, trying to focus on something—anything—other than this man.

'Do you live here?'

'I'll ask the questions.' He turned to face her, gaze narrowed. 'Who are you?'

She opened her mouth to answer that, then faltered. For three long, miserable years, she'd been The Senator's Wife. That was how she'd been defined by her husband, and everyone she'd come to know. Genevieve, as a person in her own right, was nothing and no one.

'Genevieve,' she answered shortly. Why give him the whole tragic story of her life? A first name was enough.

And it appeared to satisfy him, as he nodded once, albeit curtly.

'And you are here, on the island, because...?'

'I crashed,' she muttered. 'The storm came out of nowhere. I was too far out at sea to turn back. Then I saw this island and made my way here...'

'You were in a boat, in this,' he said.

'Well, there was no storm when I set out,' she repeated. 'Or I would never have come so far from the mainland.'

Another grunt, this time the derision was abundantly obvious. 'It is January—you cannot go two weeks without a storm like this.'

'Yeah, well...' She tapered off, hating that he was right. Hating that she felt stupid, and worthless, just as she had almost her whole marriage. The weather had been unseasonably warm, right up until that afternoon. 'I thought it would be fine.'

He crossed the room then with easy athleticism to what she now saw was a rudimentary kitchen. Everything about this cabin was rustic to the extreme. The fact it had electricity and running water were the only saving graces. She watched as he removed a can from a small cabinet, then used an old-fashioned opener to take off the lid. He grabbed a fork from the bench and stalked over to her. 'Eat this.'

She stared at it, frowning, her nose wrinkling at the smell. 'Tuna fish?'

'It's good for you.'

There was something about the statement that drew a small smile to her lips, despite the desperation of her situation. He didn't really seem like someone who'd follow nutritionist accounts on social media or something.

'It will fill you up,' he added.

'It's cold.'

'This isn't a five-star hotel.'

'I hadn't noticed.'

'Hey, if you've got complaints, you're welcome to take your chances out there.' He gestured to the windows again.

'I thought you didn't want my death on your conscience?'

'I don't. So eat something.'

And yet, perhaps in a concession to her, he began to fill a small pot with water and set it on the gas stove—which reminded her a little of the Bunsen burners she'd used in high school science lessons.

She pulled her hair over one shoulder, running her fingers through the ends, squeezing it into the towel, careful not to let the fabric part and reveal her naked body.

There was a small fridge beside the bench and as she watched, he removed coffee from it, and then cream. She dug the fork into the tuna and speared some flakes, lifting them to her lips with a grimace of distaste. She'd never been a huge fan of canned fish, but desperate times...because he was right. She was absolutely ravenous. Now that the shock of the day's events had worn off, she realised she hadn't eaten since that morning, when she'd grabbed an apple on her way out of the door of her hotel. She had intended to spend a few hours sailing around the Aegean, perhaps stopping at a populated island for lunch, if she felt like it, before going back to the mainland. Instead, she'd wound up stranded in a stone cabin in the middle of the woods, God only knew where.

'Who are you?' she asked as he tipped a little coffee

into a cafetière and then filled it with the boiling water. His hands were proportionate to the rest of him—which was to say, huge—and as he replaced the lid, she was reminded of a giant, handling a human's possessions.

He pulled a mug from a drawer and began to fill it with coffee, before he added a generous amount of cream.

'You have cream,' she said, blinking at him. 'Is there a shop on the island?'

He arched a single, thick dark brow, cynicism on his face as he strode towards her, mug held out. She took it very carefully, not wanting their fingers to brush. Her side still felt tingly from when his arm had brushed against her in the shower, and she had no need to feel that all over again.

His smirk showed that he'd recognised her gesture and understood her reasoning for it. Well, so what? Why shouldn't she hesitate to touch a strange, enormous man?

'No.'

She frowned, almost having forgotten her question.

'Once a month, supplies are sent over. The cream is long life.'

'Oh.' She nodded slowly, considering that. 'But there must be other homes? Other people?'

'Not unless they have trespassed, like you.'

She closed her eyes against that accusation. 'I was blown here by the storm.'

'So you've said.'

'Do you actually think I'd be stupid enough to wilfully come to this place? It took me hours to get to this cabin, and it's a miracle I didn't fall off a cliff or get eaten by a bear. I mean…truly. This is *not* how I saw my day going.'

He stood in front of her, hands on hips, face giving

nothing away. Then, slowly, those dark grey eyes roamed lower. Starting at her eyes, before dropping to her lips, and then lower still, as though he was picturing her naked beneath the towel, before landing on her legs.

By the time he spoke, she was so flooded with heat that she could hardly hear him over the ringing in her ears. And damn it, how she hated that her body was, against common sense and her wishes, responding to him. How on earth could she find his slow, insolent inspection *hot*?

Although, it didn't take a psychology degree to work that out. Her marriage had been ice-like, in the end. Her husband had spent all his time seducing other women, delighting in letting Genevieve find out about his affairs, and lording it over her that it was her fault he'd strayed. Her frigidness. Her lack of responsiveness to him. Her lack of experience and skills. Her failures as a wife that had led him to seek comfort in the arms of other women.

'You're injured.'

She glanced down at her legs and saw the grazes, and, on one of her thighs, a deep cut. She ran her finger over it, wincing as a sharp pain radiated through her body.

'I fell,' she murmured, as much to herself as him. 'A few times.'

'At a later point, we will discuss further how incredibly stupid it was to take this many risks with your life. Stay there.' Her jaw dropped at his rude, insulting comment, even when it was so easy to believe it, courtesy of her husband's conditioning.

He crouched down by the bed and removed a decent-sized box, which, when he opened it, she gathered must have been a medical kit. He removed a small bottle of disinfectant, some gauze and bandages.

She'd been so anxious to avoid touching him, and, despite the way memories of her husband's insults had doused the strange flickering of desire, she still suspected that if he were to reach for her, she'd catch fire.

'I can do it,' she said, holding out a hand for the supplies.

'Drink your coffee,' was all he said, crouching at her feet, and pouring some of the disinfectant onto a gauze pad. His eyes lifted to hers and the whole world seemed to start spinning, faster than she'd ever thought possible.

She opened her mouth to say something, to insist that she do her own treatment, but then he touched her leg, and she closed her eyes on a wave of something joltingly warm. Desire. She wasn't sure she'd ever felt it before—and for a long time, she'd believed she *couldn't* feel it. So despite what she knew she should do, in this situation, she found herself sitting there, breath held, as this beast of a man tended to her wounds with all the gentleness and care of Florence Nightingale.

CHAPTER TWO

IT WASN'T UNTIL his fingers had brushed her naked flesh in the shower that he realised he had barely touched another human being in years. Let alone a naked woman. Not since his wife had died and he'd buried her. On that day, there'd been hands to shake, hugs given. But he'd left mainland Greece afterwards, coming here, not caring if he lived or died.

When he went to Athens occasionally for work, he barely saw anyone from his old life. Not his friends, not her family. No one who might look at him and try to make him 'feel better'. He wasn't interested in that. When Theo came to the island, they shook hands, then set about the business of managing Nikos's extensive financial interests. For all that Nikos had taken himself to the edges of earth, he still oversaw the most critical investments and opportunities, using Theo as a trusted right hand, the manager he relied on as a conduit to his old life. He was the one person Nikos allowed behind the veil, to see him, his life, to understand his headspace.

Besides Theo, he was almost completely isolated, and up until about twenty minutes earlier he would have said, without hesitation, that he wasn't interested in ever seeing or touching another woman again. Certainly not in being intimate with one.

He now knew that to be a lie.

There was no other explanation for the blood that was pounding in his ears, the way his cock was growing hard beneath his shorts, the way fingers that were treating her wounds fairly *ached* to wrap around her calf and hold her there, before tugging gently to part her legs, so he could move his fingers higher, to brush against the sweetness of her sex. Her breasts were right in front of him, though hidden by the towel, and he wanted to take his other hand and pull the fabric away, revealing her to his hungry gaze, before his mouth tasted every single inch of her.

The betrayal of his late wife, Isabella, was like a blade in the gut, but it did nothing to stem his awareness of this woman—Genevieve. Nothing to curtail his desire and the white-hot burst of need overtaking his body, one cell at a time. Besides, desire was simply that: his body's involuntary response and recognition of another. It didn't mean anything, except that he'd been celibate way too long. Solitary and alone, not missing the touch of another, nor the contact and companionship of people. But that wasn't to say he was made of stone, and he would have needed to be not to notice the softness of her skin, the supple, athletic tone of her legs, the light caramel tan to her skin.

Once upon a time, in almost another universe, he would have found her attractive. More than attractive, he'd have said she was beautiful. From her raven-dark hair to wide-set, pale blue eyes, straight nose with a little ski jump at the tip of it, and soft, pouty pink lips that were currently held apart, showing surprise. Awareness.

Yes, he felt it, not as a man might when stirred in a

void, but rather, when the same fires of need were burning in his opposition. He felt them spark off each other, rather than simply beneath his own skin.

And then, he did let his fingers trail higher, over her smooth flesh, towards the deep cut in her leg.

'This should have stitches,' he muttered, pleased he still sounded disapproving, despite the torrent of need that was flooding him every bit as quickly as the skies had opened up this afternoon.

Her throat shifted as she swallowed, and he imagined pressing his mouth there and tasting her, sucking until her skin darkened and he left a little mark of his own on that flawless neck. She shivered, perhaps in response to the intensity of his gaze, yet he didn't look away. His finger traced around the cut as he forced his eyes to return to their inspection. Goosebumps lifted over her legs, and his lips shifted in a mocking half-smile.

'Cold?' he asked, though he knew the answer to that. The fire was raging, and they were close enough to be almost too hot. Her goosebumps could be for one reason only.

'What do you think?' was her spirited reply, so he stood and turned his back to conceal something he hadn't felt in a very long time. An actual smile. It was quick. A flash on his lips, before he managed to capture it and smother it away again. After all, what right did Nikos have to feel amusement, particularly at the hands of a beautiful woman?

'I think you would be better off just about anywhere but here,' he muttered as he opened the medical kit again and removed the Steri-Strips. When he turned to face her, she was staring at him not with fear, so much as undisguised curiosity.

'Who are you?' She repeated an earlier question, one he'd instinctively shied away from.

This was his bolt-hole, and it remained that way because very few people knew he lived here. The 'reclusive billionaire' was an apt moniker, in many ways, though it made it sound as though he had a choice in his reclusiveness. When the truth was, he was simply living the life he had earned. The life he deserved. He had caused his wife's death, after subjecting her to years of abject loneliness.

His fate was to share in hers.

He knew the speculation that went on about his life. In business circles, certainly, but even, from time to time, in the society pages. Particularly if he happened to be spotted back in Athens or further afield for any period of time. He had no interest in giving this woman any more information than was necessary.

Then again, she too had stuck to her first name, so he heard himself offer, 'Nikos.'

'Nikos,' she repeated, and something like a shiver ran the length of his spine at the way she turned the two simple syllables into warmed honey. Her American accent disappeared on the Greek word, so he itched to teach her some others. 'And you live here?'

She'd asked him that earlier, too.

He nodded once as he strode back across the room and stood before her, aware that his cock was at her eye height, and that he was growing harder by the minute. So what? Let her see what was happening to him, let her know that she should keep her distance. He was a lit fuse, apparently, and the last thing he wanted was to act on it.

Yet with the slightest invitation from her, he wondered if he'd be helpless to ignore his body's deep, carnal cravings. Though he'd been celibate since Isabella's death, it was less about a sense of betraying Isabella and more about his single-minded determination to deny himself even that pleasure. Never again would he look at another woman in a romantic sense; never again would he allow a woman to care for him, love him, or marry him. He didn't deserve any of that. And up until this moment, he'd never once been tempted.

He heard her sharp intake of breath and knew she'd noticed. Dropping his head to hide whatever expression his features twisted into, he crouched down and lightly touched her injured leg. 'Does it hurt?' His voice was gruff.

'I—'

When he looked up it was to see shock on her face. Confusion, too. Not fear. Not even uncertainty so much as wonder. Slowly, she reached out, her brows quirking closer together as she let her finger hover in the air a little to the right of his cheek and then, with another quick intake of breath, to glance over his jaw. So softly it was feather-light, so he leaned into her hand. He didn't want her tentative touch. If anything were to happen between them, it should be fast and rushed, born purely of need. Not gentle. Not inquisitive. Not a precursor to anything other than wild, animalistic sex, as desperate as the storm raging around the cabin.

'Nikos,' she said, frown deepening, as though his name held some secret, or explanation, to what she was feeling. He unfastened the Steri-Strips and gently pressed them over her wound until it stitched closed. Then he reached for the bandage and began to wrap it around her leg, his fingers brushing the backs of her thighs, then the front, needlessly touching her bare skin, until the gash was covered, and he sealed the end of the bandage to keep it in place.

Her finger stayed on his jaw, her frown in place, as he worked, and when he was finished he looked up at her. He had denied himself every pleasure for a long time, but, God help him, this woman who'd stormed into his cabin was like a vixen, drawing him in, making him want something he'd easily resisted for years.

'If you keep touching me like that, Genevieve, I will want to take you to bed. Is that what you want?'

Her breath exploded from her lips on something like an anguished cry, and her eyes fled to the double bed in the room.

It was a form of madness. What else explained the way he was suggesting sex to a woman who'd blown in with the wild Etesian winds, not an hour earlier?

'I don't even know you,' she said, taking a huge gulp of her coffee. He hadn't realised she was still holding the mug with her other hand. He reached for it, and now she didn't have time to delicately arrange her fingers so they were out of his way. He curved his hand over hers—so much larger, it was the only choice.

'That's not an answer.' And he knelt then, dangerously close to the middle of her legs, so their eyes were almost level. Still, he looked down on her, because of his height, and when she glanced up at him, the towel that had been held in place only through the hand that also held her coffee fell down a little, revealing a hint of her creamy, naked shoulder.

'Genevieve.' His voice was a command, a demanding, insistent plea. He needed her to put an end to it. He was too far gone to listen to common sense, but if she said a single word to dissuade him, if she offered even a hint of opposition, then he would stand and walk away—right out into the storm, if need be.

Growing up as large as he was, Nikos had learned the truth of his strength from a young age. He could easily overpower almost anyone—man or woman—and he had never once used that strength to his advantage. Not in a fight with a man, and never, ever in sex with a woman. The idea repulsed him.

It was always a woman's choice, a woman's pleasure, a woman's needs.

But it was with the greatest willpower in the world that he held himself still, in a kind of sexual purgatory, waiting for her to say something, to give him some indication of what she wanted, even when he knew he should deny himself Genevieve, no matter what.

Except, he *knew* what she wanted. He could see it in the tremble of her body and feel it in the finger that was still tracing the line of his jaw—it was whether or not she was ready to admit that, to either of them.

'I will not touch you unless you ask it of me,' he said, the words dragged from him as he pushed past the final barrier of his internal struggle. 'You do not need to be afraid.'

'I'm not afraid,' she said, but her eyes dropped lower, and her hand pulled away. 'Thank you for taking care of me.'

Her voice was suddenly meek and, despite her words, it seemed almost that she was scared. He stood, and, true to his inner monologue, strode towards the door, pausing only to retrieve a handgun he kept on his bedside table, before making his way out of the house and into the storm. Suddenly, it seemed like the most imperative thing in the world to get Genevieve off his island, to hell with anything else. His helicopter was the beginning and end of that, and, even though he knew he could not take off until the storm cleared, he needed to sight the damned thing, like a talisman. Only then could he take comfort from the certainty that she would be out of his hair just as soon as the storm passed. That he could let her go without succumbing to temptation. Without giving into a pleasure he didn't deserve to ever feel again.

Genevieve's clothes were saturated, so she'd tentatively sifted through his clothing—not that there was much of it—and removed a long-sleeved shirt and pulled it on. She couldn't just sit around half naked: not when her whole body was suddenly a livewire of sexual need. God, but this man was smouldering!

And all this time, she'd thought herself totally asexual. That was an easy thing to believe, when her husband's touch had left her cold. At first, she'd thought pleasure would develop from intimacy, and then she'd at least hoped that some kind of emotional satisfaction would follow sex. But it was never a solution, never anything other than an act she came to loathe. Particularly once she knew he was sleeping with other women. Women who were beautiful and confident, and no doubt vampy in the bedroom, who could be everything he wanted.

She had no idea if she'd always been like this. A slavish dedication to her journalism degree had meant she'd never really dated before meeting James, and then he'd overwhelmed her with his attention, flattered her and seduced her with promises of the life they'd lead, so that the struggle she'd known since her father's death had suddenly seemed like a distant dream.

Throughout their marriage, she'd come to accept that it was just her. She'd even come to pity her husband, to be glad that he'd cheated. At first, he'd kept the affairs private, and she'd pretended to turn the other cheek. But when the headlines had started, and the media had begun to reach out to her for quotes, she'd had to face his infidelity head-on.

Genevieve was midway through making another coffee when the door blew in and, with it, Nikos—whatever his last name was—all wild and wet, just as she'd been when she'd first arrived. His clothes were plastered to his body and her eyes fell to the gun in his hand. She couldn't look away as he stalked across the room, replacing the gun on the bedside table and saying to her, without looking in her direction, 'It is only in case of wild animals.'

Of course it was. And it was a wise precaution, going by the noises she'd heard as she'd climbed through the forest.

Then he turned to face her and, without looking away, without offering an excuse, began to peel his wet shirt from his body, leaving him standing there in just a pair of shorts. Her eyes were as plastered to him as his clothes had been a moment earlier, and her mouth was suddenly bone dry.

'The way off the island has been damaged by the storm.'

Her eyes widened and her pulse quickened. Getting off

the island hadn't even really occurred to her. That was to say, it hadn't occurred to her that it wouldn't be as easy as clicking her fingers and calling some kind of water taxi.

'Oh, but there must be a way—'

His eyes narrowed. 'Of course.'

'Okay, good.'

'When the storm clears, I'll arrange it.'

'But can't I call someone now?'

He raised his brows. 'There is no point. No one can reach the island until this clears.' He gestured to the window.

'How long have you been here?' she asked, looking around before her eyes jerked, of their own volition, back to his body.

'Three years.'

She gasped. 'How on earth can you live like this? You must be crazy.'

Yet, he didn't seem crazy, so much as…broken, like some kind of Greek Heathcliff, all tortured and seeking solitude as a result of that torture. She couldn't say why she felt that, only that the image was set in her mind and couldn't be loosened.

He looked around. 'Is there a problem?'

'It's just very sparse.'

'It doesn't bother me.'

'What do you eat?'

He lifted his shoulders. 'There is plenty of food.'

'Tuna?'

He simply held her gaze, without answering, then said, 'I'm going to get undressed, Genevieve. If my nakedness offends you, please look away.'

She *knew* she should look away. Turn her back, give

him some privacy, or suggest he use the bathroom. But instead, she stayed right where she was, incapable of doing anything but stare as his big hands pushed into the waistband of his shorts and slowly nudged them lower. She wasn't surprised by his masculinity now—it was burned into her brain—but it overheated her in all the same ways it had before. She just hadn't realised it then—too many feelings were jamming against her waterlogged mind.

His legs were so broad and muscled, as though he ran, every day. She stared at him, completely overwhelmed by the attraction that was flooding her veins.

'Would you like to touch me, Genevieve?' As he asked the question, he took a step towards her, so her eyes lifted to his face, drugged by the silver-grey of his eyes. 'Would you like to feel my body?'

Yes, every cell in her body screamed. She wanted that. She wanted that badly. No, she *needed* it.

She gasped at the realisation that this was so completely out of her control.

'I'll tell you what,' he suggested, voice blanked of emotion, even when she could see the intensity in his features and knew that he was not unfazed by this at all. 'I will stand here for one full minute. You can touch me, or you can walk away. The choice is yours.'

And he came to stand so close their toes brushed, and her body surged with white-hot need at his proximity.

'I don't know you,' she said, tremulously, catching the way his lips pulled in an almost ghoulish smile, revealing his straight white teeth.

'Does that mean you cannot want me?'

She bit into her lip, not sure how to answer that. She'd always presumed romance and connection were prerequisites for good sex, but that had been far from the case in her marriage.

And that was what finally convinced her to act. It was almost as though she'd been handed this opportunity on a silver platter: to explore a side of herself she'd always felt wanting. That she'd been ashamed of, in her marriage, because she couldn't rouse even a hint of sexual interest.

And here was a stranger, offering himself to her, with no strings, and no need for any personal information to be exchanged. God knew her heart was far too battered, her trust too often betrayed, for Genevieve to ever seek out another relationship. The little girl who'd once dreamed of white picket fences and a brood of happy little children at her feet had died a long, slow, tortured death in the face of her husband's cruelty—Genevieve would never want those things again, and certainly never trust another person to deliver them to her.

'What does it mean if I do want you?' she asked, needing him to spell it out though.

'It means nothing,' he answered. Words that were music to her ears.

Slowly, she let her hand shift outwards, to his hip, first, curving around the firm, muscled flesh there, warm despite the fact he was wet from the storm. His breath hissed from beneath his teeth.

'Not like that,' he ground out, and she jumped back, the criticism evoking every single atom of failure that had thrived during her marriage. But he stepped after her, taking her hand, and pressing it more firmly to his side. 'Do not be shy, Genevieve. I am yours to touch and take, as much as you want tonight. For as long as the storm rages, we can indulge this fantasy. After that, we need never see one another again. Yes?'

With her heart pounding in her ears, she nodded, and this time, when her spare hand reached for his other hip, it was like the creaking open of a gate, the pushing open of a door—on the other side, she didn't know what she'd find. Only she knew she couldn't wait to find out…

CHAPTER THREE

IT WASN'T FAIR to make comparisons, but how could she not? He was so different from James. Where James had slid into his late thirties with a definite paunch and softness around his middle, he was also around Genevieve's height, and his skin had that 'Washington tan', all waxy and pale, courtesy of too long spent indoors.

There was nothing virile about him, at all. Nothing that made her feel as though she'd wandered into Tarzan's lair and was ready to be his Jane. Unlike this man, who simply screamed 'man mountain' with every breath he took.

I am yours to touch.

Well, she didn't need to be told twice. Even if she wanted to stop, she wasn't sure she could. Not when he stood so perfectly still, except for the rise and fall of his rugged chest, with each breath, that showed how her exploration was affecting him. As if she needed further proof of that, with his erection huge and hard between their bodies. Her cheeks flamed as she imagined reaching down and grabbing him there, curving her fingers around his length and feeling that warm hardness in the palm of her hands. The intimacy of that! It took her breath away.

Instead, she let her fingers stay where they were, at his hips, for a long time, as she steadied her breath and tried not to pass out from the delirium of being able to do this, and knowing it meant nothing. That it changed nothing!

When the storm cleared and she got off this island, she'd still be herself—divorced, alone, but at least free of her manipulative ex-husband and all men everywhere. This was a slice out of time, a bubble they'd allowed to envelop them, a moment of shared insanity that Genevieve had no intention of resisting.

Her hands moved of their own accord behind his back, fingers splayed wide as one moved higher, and the other lower, to the curve of his muscular buttocks, and lower still, to curve around one cheek. He cursed softly in his native tongue, and her eyes widened at the sheer passion that infiltrated the word. Making her feel as though he'd never known anything quite so perfect as this. Making her feel as though she were the beginning and end of everything he'd ever wanted, even when she knew that wasn't true.

She had no idea what had brought him to this island—nor did she want to know. That wasn't what this was. It didn't matter to Genevieve if he was someone who made a habit of seducing women, or if he did this rarely. She didn't care if he had a string of girlfriends in his past. None of that mattered. He wore no wedding ring, and for this night, he was hers, just as he'd said.

She didn't even need all night, she thought with a flicker of her lips, as she swayed her body forward so her breasts brushed against his chest. Flames exploded through her, starting at her nipples and quickly eradiating her entire body. Her eyes widened in surprise.

'I didn't know...' she said, then quickly tapered off at

what she'd been about to admit. That she hadn't known anything, ever, could feel this good.

He caught her chin with one hand, tilting her face up to his, so their eyes locked and his stormy sky gaze searched hers. 'Do you want me to touch you, *koukla*?'

Her skin flushed at his use of the unfamiliar word, but also at the question. She wanted him to touch her, yes. She just didn't have the confidence to say as much. How she hated her ex-husband then, for what he'd taken from her. For how much he'd undermined her, and made her doubt herself as a sexual being.

'I—'

His finger lifted higher, to trace the outline of her full lips. 'It is an easy yes or no question.'

'Easy for you, perhaps,' she whispered.

His eyes roamed her face with lazy indolence, as though he were reading her like an open book. She stood there, incapable of looking away, of shrugging off his gaze. Incapable, too, of hiding her thoughts, she suspected, because a moment later he said, 'Will you tell me "no", if you want me to stop?'

She sucked in an uneven breath and nodded slowly.

'I need to hear you say it,' he said, but his body moved closer, so his erection pressed against her. She swallowed past a strange tightening in her throat.

'Yes,' she said, the word barely a whisper. But it was good enough for the man in front of her, whose eyes flared at the verbal consent. His hands fell to the bottom of the shirt she wore, and he moved quickly to remove it, halfway ripping it over her head to reveal her naked breasts, so she didn't have time to feel self-conscious or embarrassed, to worry about the flaws her ex-husband had been all too ready to point out. Breasts that were too small, for example. She'd been ashamed, for so long, but the way Nikos's eyes fell to and devoured them almost as though they were the answer he'd been seeking all his life…everything inside her flared to life. And it only got hotter when he swore, as if he almost couldn't bear it.

'Christos,' he murmured, dropping his head then, to whisper against the indentation of her jawline. 'Were you sent by the gods to torment me?'

She didn't have enough mental acumen left to ask him what he meant. Besides, in the small part of her brain capable of any kind of thought, she wondered the same thing. Was he a creation of her mind? Had she, in fact, crashed on the shore and fallen into a state of delirium? Surely that made more sense than this…

'Am I tormenting you?' she asked as he dropped his mouth lower, to her décolletage and then to her breast, tracing lines across it with his tongue before drawing one nipple into his mouth and sucking on it hard enough to make her groan as ecstasy overtook her completely. No one, *ever*, had made her feel like this. Stars literally flooded her eyes, making everything in the room sparkle with silver and gold, and her hands went, of necessity, to his shoulders, clinging to him there for dear life.

'You are everything I shouldn't want,' he said, making her wonder why, yet she couldn't ask the question.

His jaw was covered in stubble and it itched her chest as he dragged his mouth to her other nipple now, but in a way that only added to her heightened sense of awareness and arousal. His hand shifted to her waist, digging into the elastic of her underpants—still a little damp from the storm—and pushing them down her legs, until she was able to step out of them.

It all happened so quickly, and he was so close, so again there was no chance to feel self-conscious of her nudity, because a moment later he was lifting her as though she weighed nothing—which she supposed to a man of his stature was true—and carrying her across the rustic cabin towards the solid bed at the centre.

He placed her down on it with a mix of urgency and reverence, and no sooner had her back connected with the surprisingly comfortable mattress than his mouth was chasing hers, kissing her in a way she'd never known she could be kissed. In a way that wasn't inquisitive or tentative, and in a way that wasn't all wet and tongue-ish, as her husband had kissed. This was the exact opposite. It was a kiss that was firm and commanding, a kiss of need that made her whole body feel alive with sensations. It was a kiss that could surely only be a beginning, because she ached for—no, needed—so much more. All of this, all of him, just for as long as the storm lasted. As if to underscore that, lightning burst beyond the window, casting the cabin in a flood of light, before the thunder rumbled right overhead. She was only conscious of it in the back of her mind though—every part of her was absorbed by this. Him. And wild, uncontrollable need.

His knee parted her thighs even as he continued to kiss her, and those hands of his, big and in control, roamed her body as if he was seeing her with his touch. Over the undulations of her small breasts, to the neatness of her waist, lower, to her thighs. Then she squawked a little at the unfamiliarity of that touch, so he lifted up and stared at her, eyes darkened by passion, and said, 'Do you want me to stop?'

She could feel the heat bursting through her face but she shook her head with a wildness that was born purely of the desperate passion he'd invoked. 'Definitely not.'

His smile surprised her, because he seemed very much like a man who didn't smile often—and she enjoyed seeing it.

His hands on her thighs were just as demanding as she'd given him permission to be, separating them so her legs were spread wide, and he stared down at her sex in a way she might have longed to hide from, if this had been anyone and anything else. But somehow knowing him to be just a stranger, who she would never see again, gave this whole encounter a surreal quality that washed away any of her usual self-consciousness and doubt.

Or maybe it was the way a sensual awareness was overtaking every part of her, so she was burning up with the wild, untamed desire he had invoked, and the only solution, in the face of that, was absolute surrender.

When his mouth shifted downward, over her flat stomach, and then lower still, to her most intimate self, and his tongue began to lash against her, she cried out, the sharp sense of pleasure tormenting her, so she arched her back and cried his name, even as the shock of his intimate kiss was pulling her out of the moment.

No one had ever kissed her there. She'd never known this. And it was sublime. Absolutely, achingly sublime.

His tongue was quick and insistent, his hands holding her legs wide when she might otherwise have brought them together, purely because the pleasure he was lavishing on her almost bordered on too intense, but she could only lie there and let him obliterate all sense and reason, as the walls of everything she thought she knew about herself and her sexuality came tumbling down, tipping her over into her very first orgasm. Her very first true sexual pleasure.

It was fast and intense and completely all-consuming, so she pushed up onto her elbows as the waves exploded over her, leaving her throbbing from head to toe with the heady rush of release. 'Oh my God,' she whispered tremulously, fighting back tears at the overwhelming realisation that she was, in fact, capable of sexual pleasure and need after all. It just took this kind of Greek god to stir it to life…

'You taste like heaven,' he muttered, and though the words were flattering, she heard something in his voice that made her pause. Something that briefly marred the pleasure and euphoria she was surfing. Because he sounded resentful. Angry, even. But why?

Whatever had caused him to speak like that, she couldn't focus on it, because a minute later his fingers were pushing inside her, digging into muscles that were still spasming from the way his mouth had tipped her over the edge.

'See for yourself,' he said, shifting a little to bring his face level with hers and kissing her so she could, yes, taste her own orgasm on his lips. It was so erotic, so raw and animalistic, so absolutely the opposite of the refined, political wife James had groomed her to be. She'd never felt free to surrender to this side of herself, even when it had become clear that James had wanted it, behind closed doors. But not from his wife.

She pushed those thoughts aside, not wanting to think

of James, not willing to let him tarnish this moment. How could she think of him, anyway, when Nikos had his fingers buried inside her and was driving her to yet another soul-tingling orgasm? How could she think of anything but this?

'Perfection,' he groaned as she cried out his name, into his mouth, tumbling over into a deep abyss, courtesy of his touch. He made her feel so good, she could almost believe him. She could almost believe she was 'perfection'. At least in that moment, and at least to him. But there was too much evidence to the contrary, and she knew at some point it would consume her anew.

'Don't say that,' she said, arching her back, silently inviting him to take more of her, all of her.

He pushed up, piercing her with his gaze for a long moment. 'Are you on contraceptives?'

The question brought with it a cacophony of sound—it was so loaded with her past. With arguments with James over conceiving a baby. He'd wanted one, she hadn't. Not yet. At first, because she'd felt too young, as though her life were yet to start. And then, because their marriage had turned toxic so quickly, she couldn't have imagined complicating it by bringing a baby into their home.

'Genevieve.' The way he said her name was laced with urgency, and she nodded.

'Yes, I have an IUD.'

'Thank God. I don't have anything. I'm clean. I presume—'

'Yes.' She blinked her eyes shut. She'd been tested around the time of filing for a divorce, when the extent of her husband's infidelity had become clear. 'I'm clean.'

'And you are okay if we—' He stared down at her, the meaning clear, even without him finishing the sentence.

Her throat felt thick as a familiar sense of panic spread through her.

'I want you,' she said, with a firm nod. But then, biting down on her lip, and focusing on a point over his shoulder, 'But I should warn you…'

'Warn me of what?'

She hesitated, hating her husband so much for the way he'd made her doubt herself. Hating him for the insecurity that was now a part and parcel of who Genevieve was. 'I'm not very good at the sex stuff.'

Nikos's surprise was evident. She saw it on his features when she risked a quick glance at his face. 'I see,' he drawled, and there was something shrewd and insightful in his gaze that made her want to curl up and hide away from him properly. 'How about you let me be the judge of that?'

But what if he judged and found her wanting? What if he made love to her and realised she was just as boring and frigid as James always said?

Ice flooded her veins, turning lava cold. But he was right there, kissing her, as if he knew she needed him to blot out those thoughts—as if he inherently understood their chemistry could do that.

Would it be enough to make the sex okay?

Or would this be yet another big, fat disappointment, for both of them?

And so what? a little voice in the back of her mind shouted. So what if it was a total disaster? They weren't going to see each other again, once she got off the island. Her humiliation would be short-lived.

At least then she'd know, anyway. If sex with this guy fell flat, then she could spend the rest of her life living as a nun, knowing that no man on earth could possibly stir her to the wondrous heat other women talked about.

'Don't say I didn't warn you,' she whispered as his hands moved back to her thighs, parting them, taking care with the bandaged leg not to hurt her. His cock pressed against her sex, parting her gently at first, so she went completely rigid and still, the old, familiar fears reasserting themselves, remembered trauma and disappointment making her brace for what was to follow.

He cursed softly and then, as if he somehow innately understood that the slower he took this, the more time her doubts would have to get a grip, he simply thrust into her in one hard, desperate movement, hitching himself deep, as far as he could, so she cried out at the rush of feeling, the absolute sensation of fullness, such that she'd never known before.

Stars formed behind her eyes and she dug her nails into his shoulder, holding on now as though, if she were to let go, she might fall right off the edge of the earth. Holding on as though he were her sole anchor in this earth.

'Okay?' he asked, scanning her face.

She couldn't talk. She couldn't think. All she knew was that this was so different from—and so much better than—anything she'd ever known.

She managed a jerky nod of her head, and then he was moving his hips, pressing into her until those waves of pleasure built in her body. Her hands traced his entire body, only he caught them, one by one, trapped at the wrists, lifting them over her head and pinning them easily right there, so she was completely his captive, a prisoner of his sexual ministrations, a willing supplicant.

'You feel incredible,' he muttered. '*Christos, koukla*, you have no idea how this feels.'

If she'd been more capable of voicing words, she might have contradicted him, but her whole body was alight with passion and heat, and her mouth couldn't possibly cooperate, so she simply closed her eyes and let the feelings wash over her, again and again, as another orgasm built, and she almost wept at the intensity of the feeling. Pleasure saturated her, and her whole body was singing. She clung onto him as wave after wave of release made her whole body tingle and explode. Then he let out a deep guttural cry in Greek as his own orgasm wrapped around them like an almighty explosion.

Afterwards, only the sound of their heavy breathing filled the cabin, almost completely drowned out by the lashing rain and rumbling thunder. The lights flickered, as though they were tempted to go out, but then stabilised. Genevieve idly traced circles along his arms, blinking up at the man who'd just made wild, abandoned love to her—a man whose last name she didn't even know!

It was so completely out of character, and so absolutely outside the agreement she'd formed with James, an agreement he had the power to hold her to by the sheer amount of debt she was in to him. In exchange for his continuing to pay her mother's medical bills—which were all in Genevieve's name—and not disclosing sensitive information about Genevieve's father that she had foolishly shared early in their marriage, she had sworn she'd stay silent and single, not doing even one interview about his infidelity and *never* being seen in public with another man. At least, not until he'd remarried, and was ready to finally let her go. His damn ego simply wouldn't permit the narrative that she'd moved on first. Despite the knowledge that she'd broken that promise, she couldn't help but smile, like the cat that had got the cream. She couldn't help it. For the first time in her life, she'd felt real sexual pleasure, and she finally understood how life-changing it could be.

Nikos, though, was pulling away from her, his body when he stood a study in tension. 'Excuse me, Genevieve,' he said, without a backwards glance, as he made his way to the bathroom and closed the door. A moment later, the shower started, and Genevieve's heart sank at the obvious, offensive rejection. It shouldn't have been a big deal, but after what they'd just shared, and how he'd made her feel, it hurt, way more than she wanted to admit. She turned her face, tilting it towards the window, and found herself praying for a break in the storm, so that she might have a chance to leave, before she did something really stupid and asked him what she'd done wrong.

CHAPTER FOUR

ALL HE COULD think of was Isabella. From the moment the madness of sexual conquest had faded and sanity had returned, his wife had been there, accusing, angry. Hurt. His failings as a husband had wrapped around him, almost choking him with the cold reminder of how he'd let Isabella down. How often he'd ignored her, how much he'd destroyed her, without realising it.

In the same way he'd denied himself the pleasures of his business, his home, his life, he'd chosen celibacy, after Isabella's death. Why should he experience this sort of pleasure, after what he'd denied her?

He hadn't wanted solace, comfort. He hadn't wanted any hint of happiness. What else explained his existence here, on the edge of the earth, living in the most austere fashion, totally without reward for his hard work? He'd built himself up from nothing, and was now one of the world's richest men, yet he enjoyed no fruits of his labour. Every part of his life was now a question of basic survival, of extreme denial.

But what he'd just done with Genevieve wasn't about survival, even though, at the time, he'd felt as though his life depended on making love to her.

He let the water pour over him, eyes closed as memories sliced through him. He tried his hardest not to think of Genevieve—it seemed like even more of a betrayal of his late wife. But for almost the first time in his adult life, Nikos was out of control. His thoughts wouldn't obey him. They kept throwing Genevieve into his mind, reminding him of her voice as she'd cried his name, of how tentative she'd been at first and then how wild. How good she'd felt. How paradoxically insecure she was.

A thousand questions arose within him, questions he wished he didn't feel. Because if he knew one thing about himself, it was that he didn't like unsolved mysteries. And with the storm trapping them both in the cabin for heaven knew how long, getting to the bottom of this woman's contradictions was tempting beyond compare.

She hadn't even realised she'd fallen asleep until an enormous roll of thunder woke her up. Disorientated at first, she rolled over and gasped at the sight of the man sleeping in the bed beside her, all bare chest and dark hair, parted lips and long, dark lashes. She had no idea what time it was—her phone was somewhere on the bottom of the ocean, and her watch had stopped working courtesy of the waterlogging it received—but there was a hint of light in the cabin, suggesting dawn was upon them.

Her stomach rolled as Nikos shifted and recollections flashed through her mind like some kind of strange film. His touch, his seduction, the way he'd made love to her. The pleasure he'd given her! Pleasures she'd never known possible, much less thought to want for herself. She pushed out of the bed gingerly, her whole body heavy with a sense of what they'd done. It wasn't painful, exactly, so much as different. She felt stretched and aware of herself in ways she hadn't been before. Even her nipples tingled as she walked across to the only window of the cabin, and the fabric of his shirt—which she'd hastily pulled on the night before, as he'd showered, like some kind of protective mechanism—brushed against her.

But those memories were there, too. The way he'd disappeared after they'd finished, pulling away from her and showering, for God's sake, rather than staying and…

And what?

Cuddling?

Well, in that sense, he was just like James. He'd never favoured any kind of tenderness. The only times they'd held hands had been when they'd been attending an event and photographers had been there. One of the youngest senators in history, having taken office just a month after his thirtieth birthday, he was obsessed with cultivating the perfect image, and Genevieve, with her long political pedigree, had been a part of that. In public, he was a doting husband. But it was in such contrast to the way he was behind closed doors, that she had started to bitterly resent the false acts of closeness. It was so performative, so empty.

Nikos was nothing like James. Where her ex-husband was superficial and obsessed with power, Nikos was a man who lived on the land. She had no idea if he'd ever had a job, or if he was a wildling, cast here by the gods, to live out his life alone and desperate. But the thought of him in a suit almost made her laugh out loud, let alone attending one of the society events her husband regularly frequented. Nikos, this caveman, making small talk?

She leaned forward and wiped one of the glass panels, removing the condensation. There had been no abatement in the storm. The sky was a leaden grey and the rain continued to fall as though the heavens had turned the tap on full power. She wasn't sure she'd ever been in a storm of this magnitude.

Quietly, careful not to wake him, she pivoted and looked around the cabin, seeing it now through fresh eyes. Last night, she'd been in a state of shock, exhausted from her hike to the cabin, and thrown completely off track by the chemistry that hummed between herself and Nikos. Now, after however many hours' sleep, she felt closer to rested. Closer to calm. It enabled her to notice things she hadn't the night before. Like the small table to the edge of the kitchen. There were two chairs, which intrigued her. Why have two chairs, if not to host another person? Did that mean there was someone else on the island? Or someone else who came to the island regularly enough to necessitate a second chair?

A frown tugged at her lips as she continued scanning the room, landing on a shelf with books and files. A curiosity, which she put down to her journalism training, had her pacing softly towards it, with one glance cast over her shoulder to be sure he was still sleeping.

What kind of books did a man like Nikos read? To her disappointment, they were almost all in Greek. With the exception of a John Grisham novel and, to her amusement, a recipe book, the rest might as well have been written in ancient Sanskrit for all they'd offer any entertainment for her. As for the files, she was dying to reach out and flick through them. Surely they'd give her some insight into who he was, and what he was doing here? Maybe he was some kind of scientist, researching the natural eco systems of the island? That would make sense, she supposed. For all they'd barely spoken the night before, she could tell he was an intelligent person. It was in his expression, his turn of phrase, his quickness of reply. Her finger pressed to the spine of one of the binders, but she knew, even as she touched it, that she wouldn't pull it out and invade his privacy by looking through it. Investigating a story was one thing, but this was his life, and these were his secrets.

If he wanted to tell her what he was doing, he would.

If he didn't, well…it would be no worse than or different from the way he'd quickly run away the night before to shower her off him. Colour stained her cheeks as she remembered the pain of that. The insult. What had been such an immersive experience for her had clearly been, on some level, disgusting for him. Or regrettable, at least. It was impossible not to feel James's rejection all over again. The husband who'd never enjoyed sex with her, who'd found her lack of arousal completely disappointing.

So why had Nikos let last night happen? He didn't seem like a man who'd get swept away by passion. To live out here, like this, he must have had incredible willpower and determination. Or have been slightly crazy, she thought with a half-smile, looking around again and startling when her eyes glanced across the bed and she saw that he was now awake, watching her with an expression she couldn't interpret…but which set her pulse alight.

'I was just looking,' she said, dropping her hand away from his files.

He stayed very still, unsettling her with the intensity of his gaze.

'I was curious,' she said, with a small shrug. 'About the kind of man who would choose to live like this.'

But it was all so strange. Last night, something older than time had drawn them together, stripping away any barriers, any constructs of society and conditioning, so they were simply two people, existing in the world for the sake of pleasuring one another. The sense of estrangement now was unbearable.

She stepped away from the bookshelf as though it had bitten her, rubbing her hands in front of herself. 'I'll put another log on the fire,' she murmured. Though the cabin had grown cooler overnight, that wasn't really at the root of her icy feeling. It was the rejection she felt, the sense that he was wishing her gone again.

'I'll do it.'

'No.' Too fast. She had no idea if he was completely naked under the sheet, but she suspected he might be, and she wasn't sure her equilibrium could take another exposure to his glorious, Greek god body. 'I can do it.'

'Do you want coffee?'

Genevieve firmly believed that the first sip of the first coffee of the day was one of life's greatest pleasures, yet she shook her head to demur. 'Let me make it.'

'It is not like you are used to,' he pointed out. 'No flicking a button on a machine.'

'How do you know that's how I make coffee?'

'Am I wrong?'

She hesitated, unable to refute his presumption. 'Well, I saw what you did last night,' she sniffed. 'I'm sure I can manage.'

He simply stared back at her, in that disconcerting way of his, as though he was thinking things he knew better than to say. She prodded the fire back to life first, choosing a large log and placing it into the embers, then using the fire poker to shift the log around until flames began to lick against its sides. Afterwards, she moved to the kitchen, exploring the burner he'd used, the pot for water. It seemed simple enough. Add heat to water, let it boil, add coffee, *et voilà*.

She turned to say as much, only to find Nikos was out of bed and standing right there, in the kitchen, all big, looming, enormous hulk of a human, all gorgeous and, thankfully, wearing a pair of shorts, so at least she was spared from whatever her reaction might have been to seeing his nakedness again.

To remembering the way that nakedness had thrust inside her and turned her world utterly and wholly upside down.

'Allow me,' he said, his eyes probing hers, and now there was something in his face that was softer. Almost gentle, except nothing about this man with his harsh lines was gentle. This was the kind of man who could kill a bear with his hands alone, who could scale mountains and probably even part the sea, she thought with a surprising flicker of amusement.

She'd never known anyone like him.

Hardly surprising, given the circles she'd moved in. A quiet childhood on the outskirts of Boston, an Ivy League college education thanks to a full-ride scholarship, and then marriage to James, which had led to a suffocatingly pretentious Washington life. No chance to use her degree—James hadn't wanted a wife who worked.

'Something amusing?'

Her eyes flicked to his. 'I was just imagining you in my normal life,' she said, honestly. 'I can't imagine you anywhere but here.'

'I don't want to be anywhere but here.'

'I wasn't offering.'

His eyes sparked to hers and the air between them crackled with something that could have been animosity or could have been desire. Her insides tightened with a mix of the two.

'You're just so…rugged. The thought of you in a suit is hard to imagine.'

'Easier to think of me naked?' he asked, the question teasing. Light in tone, in a way she hadn't heard from him before. Her lips quirked but when she glanced at him, he was busying himself making coffee, back turned to her.

There was no comfortable armchair to sit in, and she didn't fancy the cold hardness of the chairs at the dining table, so she padded back to bed and sat gingerly on her side of it, propping the pillow behind her to create a sort of headrest.

'Do you work?'

He glanced over his shoulder then turned properly to face her as he waited for the water to boil.

'Yes.'

She nodded slowly. 'Are you some kind of botanist?'

At that, he actually burst out laughing. 'No, I'm not a botanist.'

'A naturalist? A scientist of some kind? Some sort of conservationist?'

'No.'

'Then, what?'

'Why would I tell you, when having you guess is more entertainment than I've had in years?'

He turned away again abruptly, reaching for the coffee and adding it to the bottom of the pot. She pleated the bedsheet with her fingers, contemplating that.

'Since you've been on the island?'

He made a grunting sound that didn't really answer her question.

'Well, if you're not a scientist, I'm at a loss. I can't really fathom why anyone would come and live out here, in the middle of nowhere. I mean, it might be nice for a holiday, I suppose, if you wanted to completely disconnect.'

He poured two mugs of coffee—yet another sign that he did entertain here, occasionally, at least—and carried them to the bed. But rather than handing one to Genevieve, he placed both on his bedside table before sitting beside her, his large frame unsettling the mattress so she was drawn a little into the middle. Towards him. Their shoulders brushed and she startled. Nikos turned towards her, his face so close their eyes sparked, and she could see all the flecks of colour in his eyes—grey, silver, and some a golden amber.

'Are you okay?'

His question caught her unawares, and seemed to tip her world even more to the side. 'I—yes.'

'After last night,' he clarified.

She glanced down at the space between them, only there was no space. Just flesh. His glorious chest was right there, and the sight of it, the memories of him, made her heart pound in a way that was unsettling to the extreme.

She'd spent so much of her marriage lying. Or, rather, faking it. Pretending to be something she wasn't, because she'd thought if she could play the part of the perfect wife, James might come back to her, and be like he had been in the beginning. She'd smothered her own discontent, she'd quietened her upset, in order to keep the peace with him.

But Nikos was a stranger, a man she didn't intend to see again, once she left the island. So why hide the truth from him? What was the downside of honesty, when she didn't actually care what he thought of her?

'Why did you go and shower last night? Afterwards, I mean.'

Even as she asked the question, though, she was surprised by how forthright it was. And proud, too. Why shouldn't she ask? As far as she was concerned, she had every right to wonder. It wasn't exactly the done thing. At least, not according to movies and romance novels.

'Did it offend you?'

She considered that. It had, but perhaps that had more to do with her past than his act. She lifted one shoulder in a half-shrug. She'd signed a non-disclosure agreement as part of her divorce. She wasn't supposed to talk about James, or he'd stop paying off her mother's medical debts. Worse, he'd do a tell-all interview about her father. While he was long gone, his political legacy lived on; she couldn't be the reason it was tarnished. Despite those threats, was there any harm in talking to *this* man, who had taken himself completely out of civilisation? What was the harm in being honest with him? Did she think he had some kind of hotline to one of the Washington papers? A gossip columnist on speed dial? The thought almost made her laugh out loud. Besides, he didn't know her last name, and had zero idea who James was.

'I'm probably too sensitive around this stuff,' she said, eventually. 'I—was recently divorced.' The words were tinged with bitterness but she supposed, to other ears, it might sound like grief. She flicked a glance at his face, briefly, but his features were set in a mask that gave nothing away. 'Coffee?' she prompted, embarrassed, because she'd revealed something vital and important, and he hadn't reacted.

He turned away from her, took hold of a mug and held it out. Genevieve tried to rearrange herself, to put space between them, but it just wasn't possible in a bed this size, with a man this weight.

She resigned herself to the fact that their shoulders would brush as they sat there.

'And you're upset?'

So he wasn't letting it go, then. She tilted her face to his. 'I'm getting used to my new reality.'

'Was it your idea, or his?'

'Mine.'

He raised his brows. 'You weren't happy?'

She sipped her coffee, closing her eyes as the pleasure of that sip wrapped around her. The last thing she expected was his feather-light touch on her face, a single finger tracing the line of her jaw, before gently angling her chin towards him. 'You were unhappy?' he repeated, eyes tracing her face, so she felt completely exposed to him.

'That's generally the reason people seek divorces, isn't it?'

A frown flickered across his features. 'Not always.'

She sipped her coffee again, purely in an attempt to cut through the connection he was forging by asking her these questions, so close, staring down into her eyes. She didn't want to feel a connection to this man, apart from, she supposed, the physical. She would never be stupid enough to put her happiness in the hands of a man again, even temporarily.

'Well, it was for me,' she said, crisply. 'My marriage was a mistake. I realised within a few months.'

'Yet you stayed.'

'It was complicated.'

'Why?'

She glanced across the room, considering that. 'There were other people in the picture. My mom. His parents. His work. Getting divorced after a few months would have been disastrous for him.'

'And staying wasn't disastrous for you?'

Surprised by his perception, she shot him another glance. There was a haunted look in his face that took her breath away. 'I thought I could fix it,' she said, finally, sipping her coffee, cheeks flaming with regret at that. How silly she'd been. How naïve. 'I thought I could fix him.'

'One person alone cannot fix a broken relationship.' It was too insightful to be anything but personal experience. She opened her mouth to say something along those lines, but he spoke first.

'It's been a long time, since I've been with a woman. To be honest, I never expected to have sex again.' Her jaw dropped at that. He was far too masculine, too virile, to even contemplate a lifetime of denial. 'I reacted badly, afterwards. I am sorry if that offended you. Believe me when I tell you, my response had nothing to do with you.' He leaned closer, so their faces were almost touching. 'Everything about you was perfect, as I said at the time.'

Her heart leaped into her throat and her pulse went into overdrive. Stars shimmered in her eyes again, all bright and silver, and, of its own accord, one hand lifted to press to his chest. Not to push him away, but to feel his warm skin beneath her palm, to touch him because he was inviting her to. He was opening the door again, to the intimacy they'd shared.

And in that moment, it was all she wanted. To banish all thoughts of James and their marriage from her mind with simple, deeply pleasurable sex with this incredibly gorgeous man.

CHAPTER FIVE

'WHAT DO YOU MEAN, AGAIN?' she asked, and inwardly he smothered a curse. Because he was showing too much. Sharing too much. He was out of practice with people. Aside from his business manager, Theo, and an occasional meeting with some of his executives, Nikos hadn't made conversation with anyone in a long time. And even then, that was business, not small talk. Not the run-of-the-mill, 'getting to know you' conversation. He'd forgotten how to hedge.

And this woman was listening with both ears, taking in everything he said and analysing it. Asking him for more than he wanted to share.

He simply stared at her, not willing to answer her question, even though he'd opened the door to it.

'You said you didn't think you'd ever have sex again. After what?'

'I just mean I'm single. By choice.'

She wrinkled her nose, clearly not sold on the line. And he couldn't blame her. Given the alacrity with which he'd dragged her to bed, he could hardly blame her for perceiving his active libido.

'Why?'

'Does it matter?'

It was like seeing her visibly retract. She shifted a little, blinking away. Another curse flew through his mind. He knew this wasn't about Genevieve. Not really. He'd just met her, after all. It was the sense of failure that dogged him constantly. The awareness that he'd once held something beautiful in his hands, had been entrusted with Isabella's life, her happiness, and he'd destroyed both. He pulled back a little, on the pretence of reaching for his own coffee and taking a long drink.

'So, how does this work?'

His chest twisted. This? Was she referring to 'them'? Hadn't he been clear about that? Sex was one thing, but as soon as the weather cleared, he needed to find a way to get her off the island. There was a radio in the helicopter, and he could call to have one of his staff dispatch a boat to collect her.

'I mean, you don't look like someone who exists on tinned tuna.'

Relief flooded his body. She was talking about his life here, on the island. Her curiosity was natural. When he'd first come here, he hadn't cared if he lived or died. He'd thrown caution to the wind, and somehow, the wind had caught him. Bringing him an abundance of food, of shelter, so, day by day, his new habitat became familiar. Home.

'The island has plenty of food.'

She arched a brow. 'Such as?'

'There's a whole ocean out there,' he pointed out.

'So you go fishing?'

He nodded once, as some of his earliest memories filtered through his mind. The smell of salt water, his father's hands, strong and capable, helping him reel in a catch that might otherwise have dragged him off the jetty, his mother smashing octopus against the rocks, until it was tender enough to char over flames. They'd fished out of desperation, to stave off hunger. On a good day, his father would catch enough to barter for something else, like eggs, or bread.

'Has anyone ever told you having a conversation with you is a little like getting blood out of a stone?'

'I'm out of practice.'

She considered that. 'Do you ever get lonely?'

'No.' Except, that wasn't completely true. He was lonely, a lot of the time. But he relished that feeling, knowing it was the punishment he deserved, because of what he'd put his wife through. His wife who had deserved so much better.

'I'd hate it.'

'Why?'

'I guess I've been lonely enough. My marriage was not happy, obviously, but, because of his job, I found it hard to meet people and really get to know them. I lost contact with a lot of my college friends. I felt alone, a lot. Now that we're divorced, I want to restart my life. I want to find myself again. I know how trite that sounds, it's just…' She tapered off and lifted her shoulders.

'It doesn't sound trite.' His own voice was hoarse. He thought of Isabella with a sense of desperation in his gut. Why hadn't she divorced him? He hadn't deserved her loyalty. Her love and devotion to a man like him had destroyed her. If only she'd done what Genevieve had and walked out. He ground his teeth together, the past too painful to spend much time on. 'What was his job?'

She hesitated for a moment. 'He's a senator,' she said,

clearing her throat a little and looking away. 'Very young, very driven, much admired.'

'I see.' The same could have been said for him. He'd been twenty-three, after all, when his private equity firm had become one of the biggest in the world. He'd worked tirelessly ever since, until Isabella's death.

'Everything was about his image,' she murmured, sipping her coffee, keeping her delicate face averted from his. He reached out without intending to, tucking a curtain of dark hair behind her ear, so he could see her better. Heat spread through his body at the simple, innocent touch. 'I guess that's par for the course for a lot of politicians, but I wasn't really prepared for the duality.'

Though they'd only just met, he could understand that. There was something so authentic and real about this woman, he could easily imagine her struggling with the other man's public persona and his private actions.

'So, fishing, huh?' she asked, clunkily changing the subject.

To his surprise, he heard himself say, 'I would go out with my father, early in the mornings, before the sun had come up. He died a long time ago, but I still hear his voice, when I cast in my line,' he admitted, turning away again, this time to put down his coffee cup. They'd been able to coax out an okay living while his father lived, but afterwards, it had been desperate.

'It's the same for me, with sailing,' she murmured. 'My father taught me, before he died. I was twelve, and it felt like the whole world had fallen down around me. My mother was never particularly maternal, but my dad…he always had time for me,' she said, smiling wistfully. 'We would go out on his boat, and he was so patient, explaining everything as many times as he needed to.' Her lips pulled to the side as she lost herself in thought. 'It's why I hired that damned boat,' she muttered. 'It was spur of the moment—a whim. I walked past the marina and saw them there, and just *felt* him, beside me, encouraging me forward. Which is stupid, really, because no way would my dad—or the ghost of him, or whatever—ever put me in that kind of danger.'

Nikos thought about that—the legend of this island, the mythical stories of its creation—and ignored the obvious parallels. He'd never believed in all that nonsense, though someone inclined that way could have said the same thing: that he had been drawn here, by fate, or something like it.

'In truth, he'd have been furious with me for setting out without checking the forecast,' she admitted, on an uneven laugh.

'The hire company should have warned you.'

'They might have. I don't speak Greek.'

He was surprised to feel a smile tugging at his lips. 'You know your phone can translate for you?'

Heat flushed her cheeks. 'I just wanted to get out on the water.' Her gaze was focused on the flickering fire across the room. 'I've felt trapped for so long, the freedom of the sea...' She turned to face him. 'It sounds stupid.'

'No,' he contradicted immediately, hating the vulnerability he sensed in her. Hating the feeling of history repeating itself. His wife had been miserable, yet he'd been too driven to succeed, to never again know the ache of hunger, the fear of poverty, to realise. He had seized every opportunity, flown across the globe, stayed in his office when she'd begged him to come home, because he couldn't imagine neglecting his business.

So he'd neglected his wife—and lived to regret it, with every part of himself.

It was because of Isabella that he was so easily able to spot the signs now, to read the self-doubt. And while he hadn't caused Genevieve's situation, he couldn't help but wonder if meeting her wasn't giving him a second chance. An opportunity to do something good for someone, for once. It would never undo the damage he'd caused Isabella, though. Nothing could, and he would carry that guilt for a lifetime, always atoning for the error of his ways. 'I understand it,' he said. 'The same is true for me, out here. There is a sense of freedom that comes of this life.'

She wrinkled her nose. 'This is a pretty extreme version of freedom, though,' she pointed out, flicking him a small smile.

He dipped his head in acknowledgement. 'It's right for me.'

Her eyes swept his face, thoughtfully. 'When did you last leave the island?'

'About three months ago.'

'Oh!' Her reaction was easy to interpret.

'That surprises you?'

'Yes, honestly. You seem almost to be carved out of the cliff face,' she admitted. 'I don't know if I can picture you anywhere else.'

'I never stay away long.'

Her fingers moved over the sheet, pleating it into neat little folds. 'Where did you go?'

'Athens.'

Her eyes flicked to his.

'Have you been?'

She nodded once. 'I flew into Athens, but I only spent one night. I'd like to go back at some point. Before I head home.' She laughed softly. 'If I ever make it off this damned island.'

'When the storm breaks, you can leave,' he said, as much as a reminder to himself as her.

'But how?'

'We'll work it out.'

'That's not an answer.'

She was right. He was being deliberately cagey, and he realised why. He liked her not knowing who he was. He liked that she didn't know about his money, his business, his empire. He liked that they were sitting here, talking as two people, with shared experiences of grief, though she wasn't aware of his. But why hide the truth from her? He was Nikos Konstantinou, and he had no intention of hiding that from her for ever. He split the difference, in the end, deciding to reveal some details without showing his full biography.

'I have a small, old helicopter in a clearing behind the cabin,' he said, voice neutral. 'I can get the radio working, once the storm stops, get someone to come over for you.'

Her eyes widened. 'A helicopter?'

He reached for his coffee, took a long drink, then glanced towards the window. 'I doubt the weather will clear today, though. You're stuck here a while longer.'

She nodded slowly. 'I can deal with that.' Her cheeks flushed pink, and it was easy to understand why. To know what she was thinking, because his mind was going there, too. They had very limited time together, and he wasn't going to waste it. He'd made his peace with the fact they'd slept together, because it was temporary and meaningless.

Except, maybe it wasn't completely meaningless. Oh, for Nikos it could never be more than a physical connection, but was it possible he could help heal the wounds her terrible excuse of a husband had created? Could he help put her back together, in the way he should have been able to do for Isabella? It would not cure his guilt, but at least it would be something. An offering to the gods of karma, a righting of the scales, in some small, desperate way.

Genevieve stared at the ceiling, cheeks flushed, body covered in a fine film of perspiration, mouth unable to form words. Brain barely able to conceive of them. What had started with coffee in bed had turned into something else entirely, and hours had passed with them exploring each other's bodies. His every touch, his kisses, his fascination with her, until a fever had gripped her and she was spiralling into a whole new dimension, unlikely to ever return to this one again. At least, not as she'd once been. This version of Genevieve was completely different. She was fire and flame, awoken and hungry. It was as if he'd turned on a pleasure tap within her, and now she knew it existed, she had to accept that it was a part of her, and always would be.

How strange to have lived her whole life with no concept that she was a sexual person. With no idea that a single touch could set her skin alight.

Even stranger to see how she'd surrendered herself to this. Because with every minute that passed, every raindrop that fell, the heavens were closer to exhausting their supply of tears, and that meant one thing, and one thing only: she would leave again. She would leave this island, return to the small coastal town she'd rented a little room in, and go on with this holiday. The 'honeymoon', she'd called it, because it was a trip she'd planned to mark a commitment back to herself. It was a way of celebrating her freedom, and the second phase of her life.

Whatever that would look like.

And whatever her 'freedom' meant, because though she'd been able to divorce her husband, he still held the strings. He was her puppet master, and would be until she was able to properly stand on her own two feet. For as long as he held her mother's medical expenses over her, Genevieve had no choice but to be the contrite, good ex-wife, toeing whatever line he asked her to. Even to come away on this holiday, she'd had to barter with him.

Anger rushed through her, catching her totally unawares, because it was something she was usually able to keep under control. Except with Nikos, somehow, he'd uncorked the passion centres of her body, so now everything was heat and flame.

She pushed up onto one elbow, so she could face him. His eyes were closed, his face held tersely, and she frowned, realising that the last time they'd made love, he'd got straight up and gone to shower. Was he thinking about doing that again?

Was he holding back, for her?

'If you need to go wash, you can,' she said, pleased her voice sounded somewhat level.

He turned to face her, eyes landing on hers and causing her heart to thud. 'That wasn't about you.'

'Wasn't it?'

He reached out, brushing a hand over her cheek. 'Where are you staying?'

She frowned, not immediately understanding.

'You said you flew into Athens. Where are you now?'

'Oh. Katanos,' she said, naming a small coastal fishing village somewhere across the Aegean. 'Do you know it?'

His smile was mesmerising. 'I grew up about thirty miles to the south. I spent time there, as a child. It's very beautiful. Why Katanos? It's not really on the tourist track.'

'No,' she agreed. 'But it's where my parents went on their honeymoon. We had a photograph of the harbour, in our lounge room, when I was a girl. I used to look at it and imagine I was a mermaid, diving deep into the ocean, losing myself in that crystal-clear turquoise water. I'm not sure when I consciously decided to come here, but after the divorce, I couldn't think of anywhere else I wanted to be. Strange, right?'

'Are you close to your mother?'

Genevieve's heart twisted. She shook her head once. 'She passed away a while ago.' She cleared her throat. 'She had a series of strokes,' Genevieve said. 'She was hospitalised for a long time, and then, one night…'

Nikos pushed up onto his elbow, so they were like bookends in bed, facing one another. 'I'm sorry.'

He frowned, eyes roaming her face thoughtfully. 'Did she like your husband?'

'James,' she said, slanting a glance at him, figuring it made sense for him to know her husband's name, seeing as they were speaking of him so often. 'My ex-husband's name is James J. Wilson the third. As you can guess from that mouthful, he's from old money. The prevailing opinion was that I was very lucky to have snagged him.' She rolled her eyes.

Nikos made a sound of disapproval.

'And yes, my mother adored him. Once upon a time, my parents had money, too. My father came from one of those political families, so, on paper, we were a good match. But in reality, I hated that life and lifestyle. It wasn't for me.'

'Your father was a politician?'

She nodded, opening her mouth to speak, then slamming it shut. She'd told James about her father, and he'd held that over her almost from that night, threatening to expose her father, to ruin his legacy. But somehow, she just knew she could trust Nikos. That he'd never, ever do something so unscrupulous. 'He was a politician, yes, with a serious penchant for gambling, which wasn't apparent until after his death. We were left with a heap of debt.' She closed her eyes. 'I can't believe I'm telling you this.'

He made a sound, querying that.

'I never talk about it.' Except for one time, and she'd lived to regret that. But with Nikos, it just felt...different.

He reached out, pressing a finger to her shoulder and shifting it downwards. 'You worship him.'

Her smile was soft. 'I suppose I do, yes. He was a kind man. I wish... His gambling, the fact he hid it all from Mom, was obviously wrong. I know he must have carried a lot of shame, and regret, but I wish he'd been honest with her. Not least because she might have been able to help him,' Genevieve added. 'So when a rich, handsome senator came into my life and started pursuing me as though his life depended on it, Mom was all too keen to buy into the whole thing. A fairy tale, she called it. I think she had a fantasy of James being able to turn us back into what we once were. Instead, it turned into a horror show.'

Nikos moved forward, so their naked bodies were connected, touching leg to leg, chest to chest. His eyes bore into hers with an intensity that took her breath away. 'Did he hurt you, Genevieve?'

'No,' she said, then frowned, because that wasn't strictly true. 'I mean, he never hit me or anything.'

'That is not the only way to hurt someone.'

And there was something about this room, this man, the flickering fire, the heavenly sensations in her body, that made her open herself completely to him. 'He was cold and cruel,' she admitted. 'Nothing I did was ever good enough for him. I was expected to be the perfect political asset and yet I constantly fell short of his expectations. Things between us…' she flushed to the roots of her hair '…in bed, I mean, were…lacklustre, and he made it clear that was my fault.'

The scoffing sound Nikos made should have warmed her, but Genevieve was back in the past, the ice spreading through her veins, so she barely heard him.

'He cheated, and blamed me. If I'd been a better wife, a better lover, more satisfying, he wouldn't have needed to stray.' She said the words with disdain, showing how little she believed them now. But at the time, when she'd been under his spell, and captive in his home, dependent on him completely, she'd taken each and every sledge to the heart, letting it shape her entire world view.

'Bastard,' Nikos ground out, his indignation bringing a small smile to her face.

'Yes.' How could she argue with that? 'At first, he was careful to keep the affairs secret, and I pretended I didn't know. That I didn't see.' Her skin felt cold and clammy. 'Then one of his mistresses went to the press. The story broke, and that's when things got really bad. Somehow, that was my fault too,' she murmured. 'I tried to leave him then, but he made it obvious he would make my life very, very difficult if I walked out.'

'Difficult how?' There was a darkness to his tone that set her pulse racing. A protectiveness that she'd never known from anyone. It wasn't until that moment that Genevieve realised how long she'd been doing this on her own, fighting all her own battles, bearing her own scars.

'Let's just say he's not someone I want to get on the bad side of.'

Nikos frowned.

'I feel so stupid,' she admitted. 'I really wanted to believe him. To believe that he loved me, that we'd live happily ever after. I bought into the fairy tale, but he was a monster.'

Nikos made another noise, and then his mouth was claiming hers, kissing her until she tasted the salt of her tears.

'You deserved so much better,' he said, with so much darkness she felt it pierce something deep in her soul, conversely letting light in for the first time in years. It didn't occur to her—how could it have?—that he wasn't really speaking to her, so much as a figment of his past. It didn't matter, anyway. The warming effect was the same.

CHAPTER SIX

THE SKY WAS thunderously grey but the rain at least stopped that afternoon, allowing them to leave the cabin. Genevieve's shoes were still damp, but she pulled them on over a big pair of thick socks Nikos had given her. She could have been tempted to stay in bed with him all day, but at the same time the knowledge that her time here on the island was limited had her wanting to see more than just the inside of his cabin—as much as she would always remember every single detail of it.

One glance from the top of the cliff towards the ocean showed the waves coming in thick and fast, the ocean too swollen to make boat travel possible yet, regardless of the storm. She ignored the slight bubble of relief at that, and what it signalled.

So, she liked being here.

She liked—surprisingly—spending time with Nikos.

That didn't *mean* anything.

It would take more than exceptional skills in bed and an interesting conversation or two to weaken the barriers Genevieve had erected around her heart and soul. Never again would she let another man permeate either. She was independent and alone. Even without James's stipulation that she stay single, this was something she intended to do for herself.

There was no hint of her small sailing boat. It had been devoured by the ocean, and a shiver ran down her spine as she imagined herself having suffered the same fate. Had she not been able to make it to this island, she would have undoubtedly been lost at sea.

She ignored the ice-like feeling wrapping around her.

There was no sense thinking about hypotheticals. She'd made it here, and she'd made it to Nikos, which seemed strangely fated, now she thought about it. She dismissed the idea, though, quickly enough. She didn't believe in anything like that. But when his hand reached down and curved around hers, pulling her away from the edge of the cliff face, back towards the cabin and the clearing around it, her whole body began to tingle in a way that definitely seemed other-worldly.

He was silent as they walked, yet a million questions flooded her mind. She realised that for all they'd spent the day alternating between making love and talking, it had been Genevieve who'd shared the most. Genevieve who'd all but bared her soul. Then again, was that really a surprise? She'd had no one to talk to about her failing marriage. No girlfriends she could confide in, and even a psychologist had been out of the question, because of James's privacy concerns.

No, it was this man, this cabin, this island and the storm that conspired to create a perfect slice away from the rest of the world. Only that bubble enabled her to be so open with him.

It helped that he was so far removed from her normal world. They would have no acquaintances in common, having obviously moved in very different circles. She could speak to him without any concerns of it becoming public, and here, well away from humanity and society, there was no risk of their liaison being discovered. It was safe, safe in a way she hadn't really understood she'd needed.

Seeing the cabin now, from the outside, without the fear of the storm bearing down upon her, meant she could regard it properly, taking in more details than she'd been capable of the night before. It was rustic in construction, but obviously very well built. Stones had been placed close together, mortared, to form the walls, and the roof was made of a sort of plaster and wood.

'It's soil and lime plaster,' he said, when she asked. 'Reinforced with sand.'

She nodded.

'I wanted to be able to use it as a second floor. In the summer, I sleep up there, some nights.'

She turned to face him, and the image he created was so incredibly romantic and earthy, so animalistic and pure, that she felt a part of her soul chipping off and coming to rest right here, in this forest, atop a mountain on a Greek volcano. 'Do you mean you built this?' Her voice emerged squeaky, but she couldn't help it. Surprise ran through her veins.

'Builders are in short supply on the island,' he quipped, but, despite having known him fewer than twenty-four hours, she had the sense he was obfuscating, intentionally concealing something from her.

'Still, that must have been quite a challenge.'

'That was what I needed, at the time.'

Why? The question died on her lips; she knew he

wouldn't answer. Not yet. She would ask it again, later, when his guard was more fully down. They walked, hand in hand, to the rear of the cabin, and Genevieve let out a small sound of surprise. Here was a vegetable garden as fully developed as any she'd seen. There were fruit trees too, some heavy with citrus.

'This is better than tinned tuna,' she pointed out.

His smile made her heart tremble. 'A little.'

At the back of the house, there was also a large freezer. 'Meat and fish,' he explained. 'Some cheeses that freeze well.'

'You're hardly roughing it, then.'

He laughed.

'Though it's not what I'd call luxurious, either.'

'It's fine for me.'

She nodded, but there was something in his statement that didn't make sense. What kind of humble mountain man had a helicopter casually parked out the back? She glanced through the forest and saw the flash of metal, and knew that was where he had it stored.

'Thinking of escape?' he asked, squeezing her hand.

'I don't think I need to escape,' she replied. 'I'm not your prisoner.'

'No,' he agreed, but his voice was flat.

They didn't walk far. The sky was inclement and, sure enough, after they'd picked their way through the forest for fifteen minutes or so, until they reached a large, verdant tree covered in spiky little orange and red balls, a few drops of rain began to fall.

'It's an Irish Strawberry tree,' he said, reaching for one and picking it.

'I've never seen that before.'

'They're quite common in Greece. There are many on the island.'

'Where exactly are we, Nikos? I lost my bearings in the storm.'

'The island is called Therasia Notia. A few nautical miles south of Psara.'

'I've never heard of it.'

'I'm not surprised.'

'How can it be empty?'

He looked at her, long and hard, then sighed. 'Because I want it to be.'

'That makes no sense.'

Rain began to fall, splishy splashy drops. 'Come on, *koukla*. Come back to the cabin.'

She walked quickly beside him, but her mind was still turning over the statement, his certainty that he could keep the island empty, at a single command.

Rain fell heavier though, and lightning began to spark in the sky once more, so she stayed quiet until they'd reached the cabin and moved to stand in front of the fire.

'Nikos,' she said, eyes lancing him, holding his gaze. She didn't need to say anything else; he understood.

'I own it,' he said, almost defiantly, as though he was challenging her. 'The island is mine, and it's empty because I wish to keep it that way.'

Her jaw dropped. Of course, she knew people who owned things like islands. Some of James's donors had been that kind of filthy, stinking rich. But even in that rarefied upper echelon, it was, in Genevieve's experience, unusual. And to keep a beautiful island like this without capitalising on its possible value?

Suddenly, she felt betrayed. It was stupid, because he

hadn't lied to her. But the image she'd had of him as some simple mountain man, existing off the land, was an illusion, disappearing like vapour before her eyes.

'I see,' she murmured, unable to keep the hurt from her tone, and hating herself for that. With James, she'd managed to hide how she was feeling. But years of play-acting had exhausted her, so now only her authentic self was on display.

'I bought it a few years ago, when I was looking to get away.'

She focused all her attention on the fire, ignoring the way he was staring down at her, as if he could read her thoughts if he stared long and hard enough.

'You just bought an island?'

'This bothers you?'

She glanced up at him. It was on the tip of her tongue to deny it but, with Nikos, it didn't feel right to hide herself. 'A little.' She sighed heavily. 'I know I have no right. It's just, you're different from what I thought.'

'Am I? Why?'

She held her hands towards the fire, seeking warmth. 'You're obviously very wealthy, for one thing. All of this—' she gestured around the cabin '—is just pretend.'

'Believe me, it's not.'

'But you could jump in your helicopter at any time and fly somewhere else.' Her eyes narrowed. 'Tell me, Nikos, do you have another home somewhere?'

A muscle jerked low in his jaw. 'This is my home.'

'You know that's not what I'm asking.'

'I have other properties, yes,' he said, eventually.

'I see.'

His brows knitted together. 'I haven't lied to you.'

He hadn't. Not really. Yet his every action had been a lie, of sorts, creating an illusion of something that didn't exist. Beneath the veneer of this rugged, wild beast of a man was someone wealthy and cultivated, civilised, who might be every bit as at home in a suit as her husband had been.

His hands caught her hips then, turning her to face him, and his features held an intensity that took her breath away. 'Who I am, on this island, is the real me. This, here. I chose this life, because it's where I belong. What does it matter that I also have business interests?'

'And money,' she pointed out.

'Yes, and money.'

'I've just known people with money. It's come to be a marker of what I want to avoid.'

'And if we were anything more than this, I might understand why you were annoyed. But true or false, Genevieve—you are leaving this island as soon as you are safely able to do so. What should it matter to you how much money is in my bank account? It changes nothing.'

She opened her mouth to argue that, to dispute it, but he was right. It shouldn't matter.

She looked down at his chest, swallowed past a strangely constricted throat. 'I'm just…wary. After him.'

'That is understandable.' His own voice sounded raw, deep and husky. It set the hairs on her arms on edge with pleasurable anticipation. 'I wasn't born wealthy. If anything, my life was the opposite. I knew abject poverty. I knew what it was like to have to make clothes and shoes last far longer than they should. I was often hungry. I knew longing and need, the struggle of not being able to have things others did, of seeing my mother make unimaginable choices, just so we would have somewhere to live.'

'What kind of choices?' she asked, momentarily thrown off course.

He stared at her, long and hard, and she could practically see his cogs turning. She could feel his internal war as he decided how much of himself he was willing to share.

'The sort of choices I would not wish on anyone,' he said, eventually, the words dragged from him. Then his voice softened. 'So what you see here, on the island, is far closer to who I am, in my heart. All the rest is just... trappings.' He sounded so grim though, so angry.

She lifted her gaze to his face, trying to make sense of it.

'Why does that bother you?'

He shook his head once. 'It doesn't matter.'

But it did to Genevieve. 'Why can't you answer?'

'Because I don't know how,' he said, finally, simply.

She blinked at him, frustration curling inside her. She knew it was partly because of her journalistic training, and partly because of who she was—the latter had made her excellent at the former—but neither looked likely to be satisfied. Nikos was closing up like a drawbridge being raised.

He moved towards the kitchen, removing things from the small fridge, leaving her looking at this man, this contradiction in terms, with the sense that, even if she had all the time in the world, she'd never properly understand him, because he was determined to keep himself under lock and key.

She knew she should have been grateful for that. It was

much harder to let herself develop fantasies around a man who kept her at an emotional arm's length. And she was no longer blind to the inherent dangers of remaining on the island. For the longer she stayed, the longer she stayed *with Nikos*, the harder it would be to remember that she never planned to let anyone else in.

Sex was sex, but, with Nikos, it was also the setting fire to her entire universe, and, with Genevieve in the centre of it, she knew that if she wasn't very careful, she was going to get burned beyond recognition.

'Okay,' she said, over-brightly. 'Let's eat. Can I help?'

He hadn't set out to hide so much of himself from her. Perhaps it had been partly because he needed to keep his private life private. His grief was his own to bear, and he had no intention of sharing it with anyone. Let alone someone like Genevieve, who might listen to his heart-break and try to make him feel better.

He didn't *want* to feel better.

Not better than this, anyway.

But *this* was temporary. This fling, or whatever it could be called, was like quicksand. Not real, not permanent, just a very temporary state of affairs. He wished he didn't know her last name, in a way, because he wanted the insurance policy against reaching out to her again. He wanted to know that when she left the island, that would be the end of it.

Because she made him feel good, and warm. In some brief moments, she even made him feel whole, and he knew he didn't deserve that.

But he hadn't expected her reaction to his statement

about owning the island. He hadn't foreseen that she would be angry with him, that she would withdraw.

He'd known Isabella for a long time—years—before they'd begun to date. He'd got a low-level job for her father, organised by a church charity that he'd gone to for food after his mother's death. He and Isabella had been thrown together at certain company functions and events. Them being a couple had grown slowly and dependably. Like building this cabin, he supposed, it had been brick by brick, bit by bit, until suddenly they were engaged and planning a wedding. For Nikos, it had made sense. He hadn't really thought about love. It had seemed an abstract concept—perhaps his childhood and adolescence had made it so.

He had already been committed to his then future father-in-law, indebted to him for the faith the older man had put in Nikos when he was starting out in his career. While it had been Nikos's innate intelligence and skill, grit and determination that had taken his career from strength to strength, it was Isabella's father who'd opened the door, giving him the opportunity to prove himself. In the end, he hadn't been able to lose sight of his goal. Each victory professionally had been the shifting of the goalposts, to work harder, achieve more. His need for success had been insatiable, born out of the flipside of that: poverty and pain.

The freezer on the island was always packed. Constant hunger still bred a sort of food insecurity for Nikos. It was strange that even now, as a grown man worth hundreds of billions of dollars, he liked knowing he had plenty of food available. Then again, on the island, it was a wise precaution.

'Do you eat everything?'

'I mean, not everything,' she said, wrinkling her nose in a way he tried not to find adorable. Sexy, beautiful and alluring were fine. Adorable was a shade of grey he didn't want to approach. 'But most things.'

'Lamb?'

'Love it.'

'Good answer.'

He ignored the warmth in his chest. She was leaving. Asap. This was no big deal.

If anything, having Genevieve here and then letting her go would be an excellent kick in the guts—a refresher course in loneliness. Because, for this short window of time, he was becoming used to company again, to the presence of someone else—a beautiful woman, no less.

While the lamb grilled, he cut up some salad, serving it on the two plates the cabin boasted, and placing it at the small table. He'd built it with Theo and himself in mind—they'd needed space to put two laptops, so they could work, on the days Theo came to the island. It was fine for a couple to share a meal but, he had to admit, he'd never been aware of the intimacy of the space before now.

Everything Genevieve did was dainty, right down to the way she ate. He watched as she delicately sliced into the meat, lifting a piece to her mouth, tasting it thoughtfully before letting out a soft, sensual moan of appreciation that made his cock hard against his pants.

Christo, but she was stunning. A vixen, sent to tempt him. And he'd fallen at the first chance. Guilt slashed him and he let it. He *should* feel guilty, for the rest of his life.

'You're a good cook,' she said, after a few mouthfuls.

'It's easy to make lamb.'

A smile quirked her lips. 'I'm impressed, anyway.'

'Do you cook?'

'I used to. I used to love it. Another thing my father taught me,' she said softly. 'We would make the most elaborate dinners. Mom had little patience for cooking, or anything domestic, so, after Dad died, I took over most of our meals, grocery shopping, that kind of thing.' She hesitated a moment, and he found himself leaning forward a little. 'But when I married James, we had someone who did all that. He…thought it was beneath his wife to cook.'

Disapproval tightened in his gut. 'Even though you enjoyed it?'

Her lips pulled to the side. 'I don't think James really cared what I enjoyed.'

He made a dark sound. How he despised that man. His cruel, thoughtless treatment of Genevieve. But was he any better? He had never wanted to hurt Isabella. He would have given her anything she asked, except his time.

'Do you have a cook?' Genevieve asked, sliding the question into the conversation in a relaxed tone. But he knew what she was doing. Trying to sound him out about his life away from the cabin. She had no idea what a nightmare it had become—how he did almost anything to avoid returning to the home he'd shared with Isabella.

He didn't sell the place, though. Nor did he change it, in any way. Like pressing his finger into a bruise, he forced himself to go back there for certain days of the year. Her birthday, their wedding anniversary. Days when he really felt he deserved to marinate in his failings as a husband—and the consequences of them.

Isabella was everywhere in their home. Her clothes still hung in the wardrobe, her shoes were neatly arranged in the shelves she'd had built to showcase them, like some kind of store. Even her toothbrush was there, in their shared bathroom.

He knew it wasn't healthy, but that was a choice he'd made. To live for ever in a state of purgatory, so that even if he came close to forgetting, to feeling like himself again, he would have physical talismans to remind him of what he'd done wrong. Of how he'd messed up.

'I'm guessing yes, given you own an island.'

He refocused his attention on her. 'Yes,' he agreed, after a beat. 'I had a housekeeper, who also did most of the cooking.'

Isabella had been a terrible cook. The book he'd given her for their first wedding anniversary had been a joke—he still had it. It was one of the few items he'd brought with him to the island—another bruise to be pushed into, to remind himself of what he'd once had, and been too foolish to appreciate. Too selfish to protect.

'What did you study at university?' he asked, turning the questions back on her, seeking temporary relief in the change of subject. With Genevieve here, he found his predilection for sadistic self-torture waning, in favour of enjoying these few days. A slight reprieve, he thought, one that was in and of itself a double-edged sword.

Because he couldn't look at this woman and want her, couldn't look at and admire her beauty, without knowing it was a betrayal of Isabella. The woman who'd deserved so much better than he'd been able to offer.

In hindsight, marrying her had been a mistake. But she'd loved him so much, and her father had desperately wanted the union. Rather than disappointing either of them, Nikos had proposed. But his focus had always been on the business, his passion entirely given over to his professional successes.

In reality, he was no better than Genevieve's husband had been. The thought sickened him, so he blanked it, focusing instead on the woman across from him and the storm raging outside, and the fact it didn't show any signs of dying down. Not that he really wanted it to.

CHAPTER SEVEN

'I COULD WATCH you lose yourself to me all day,' he said, darkly, lifting his head from between her legs to stare up into her eyes. Genevieve felt heat flush her cheeks—now not from the pleasure of what he was doing to her body, but because of the words he gave her.

'I—' The sense of embarrassment had her quickly shutting her mouth, flattening the admission she'd been about to make.

'You?' he asked gruffly, drawing his mouth to her thigh and kissing her there. Her fingers reached down and tangled in his dark hair.

She arched her back as a thousand and one fantasies whispered through her. What the hell? Wasn't honesty her new policy? 'I never knew sex could feel like this.'

He lifted up to stare at her then, bracing himself on his elbows.

In for a penny, in for a pound…

'Until I met you, I'd never actually, um, you know… finished.'

'You mean, come?'

He was teasing her, but there was something dark in the backs of his eyes, a look that spoke of repressed anger. She nodded her head quickly, dropping her gaze. His body moved then, shifting up hers, until his hard cock was at her sex and the weight of him was on top of her, all rough and muscly. 'Your husband—' he spoke darkly, thickly '—is a useless bastard.'

She closed her eyes, a strange sense of loyalty—ingrained rather than deserved—making her want to argue that. But how could she? Objectively, he was right.

'You deserve to feel this often and always. Your husband should have known better.' And he kissed her then as he took her, in the way she desperately wanted: hard, fast, as though they were the last humans on earth and this act alone could save humanity. All thoughts of James fell from her mind as she revelled only in this.

Genevieve woke early the next morning. Her dreams had been a strange mixture of the past. Meeting James, their wedding, her mother's strokes, and death, the hospital, the island, the storm that had brought her here. She tried to turn over and go back to sleep, but her brain was too active, replaying things she would sooner forget. James's affairs. The headlines. The media's calls to her—even from former students of her alma mater, who'd thought that might give them an 'in' with her. The feeling of shame and embarrassment that the whole world must know her own husband didn't even love her.

Eventually, she gave up on sleep, and paced quietly across the cabin, setting a pot of water on to boil, then making her way to the bookshelf. She'd never been much of a crime fan, but she picked up the John Grisham book and read a few pages, before placing it softly back on the shelf and, out of desperation, reaching for the only other English language book available. Even if it was a recipe book.

She lifted it out, fingers flicking through the recipes, until something fell loose from the pages and dropped to the floor. She bent to pick it up at the same time she became conscious of Nikos moving. Standing and quickly stalking towards her. But it was too late; she'd already seen it. Though it made little sense.

For within the pages of the recipe book, a single photo had been stored. Of what looked like Nikos on his wedding day. Her fingers trembled as she picked it up and stared at it, at the beautiful woman in the photo, with bright blonde hair and huge green eyes, and the kind of smile that could light up a whole room. The woman was looking up at Nikos as though he was the centre of her entire universe.

'Give that to me.' His voice was hard, roughened by something—secrecy, pain, anger?

Genevieve's stomach rolled.

'Are you married?'

He took the photo from her fingers, and she offered no resistance, but she quickly stepped back, putting space between them.

His lips formed a grim line; he looked almost unrecognisable. No, he looked as he had that first night. Unapproachable and barely human.

Her whole body felt knotty and strange. If this man was married, if she'd unwittingly become the other woman, a source of pain to another long-suffering wife, as she'd been, she could never forgive herself.

'No.'

Her heart twisted as her eyes lifted to his.

'But you were?'

He reached for the cookbook next, and now when he opened it, she saw an inscription on the front page, where he neatly placed the photo before closing the book and sliding it back on the shelf. He moved towards the kitchen, to make coffee, but his back was ramrod straight, his shoulders squared. Tension emanated from him, no matter how he tried to hide it.

'Damn it, Nikos, don't you think I deserve to know?'

'My marriage is my private business.'

It stung. It stung more than she could ever possibly admit in that moment, and more than she could or would show him.

James had hurt her so many times, with his cruelty and his coldness, and she'd become an expert at hiding that. As soon as she'd realised he was trying to hurt her, she'd refused to give him the satisfaction. It had been a sick, gruelling game, and she'd hated playing it, but at least it meant she was match fit for this encounter.

'Suit yourself,' she muttered, moving towards the window only because it was the furthest point from Nikos she could get. Her eyes swept across the view without her realising at first how far she could see. But then, it dawned on her. The sky was clear. The sun was shining.

'The storm's broken.' And she wasn't even regretful about it. Anger and wariness were taking over everything else. The sense that she'd put herself on the line, sharing everything with this man, even when she'd signed an agreement to prevent her from doing so, and he'd never once told her about his own marriage. His wife.

'Yes. It stopped raining a little after twelve.'

She turned to face him, and just stared. Because they

both knew what this meant. They'd promised she would leave as soon as it was safe to do so. Had anything changed? Maybe she'd thought so, at some point over the last two days. But somehow, finding out about his marriage, that he hadn't told her, made Genevieve doubt the sincerity of everything they'd shared. And she'd been burned by falseness once before.

Burned badly enough to never trust again. At least, that was what she'd thought. But she had let Nikos in. She had started to trust and *like* him. To feel…things that were too complicated. It was a salient reminder of why she needed to avoid relationships altogether. Hurt was the inevitable conclusion of caring.

And yet still, there must have been a part of her that hoped he might want her to stay longer, that might suggest another day and night, because it took a huge effort not to react when he said, 'I'll radio Theo to send a boat for you. It shouldn't take more than an hour.' And with that, coffee made, he stalked past Genevieve and out of the front door, presumably to the helicopter's radio.

Her heart sank to her toes, even as she told herself she was glad. This was definitely for the best.

He placed the call to Theo then deliberately stayed away from the cabin, until he saw the boat on the horizon. He knew that if he went back, he'd tell her about Isabella. About his marriage, his regrets, his guilt, and that she might look at him with those soft blue eyes and try to convince him not to be so hard on himself.

He'd heard it often enough from his father-in-law, who'd insisted Isabella had loved Nikos, had understood his drive and commitment. He'd heard it from Theo, who'd known both Isabella and Nikos for years. He didn't want to hear it from anyone else. Couldn't they understand?

He'd neglected his wife to the point of her death. He had been the cause of her misery and finally her loss. But perhaps there was another reason he didn't want Genevieve to know. Because he didn't want her to look at him and see that he too had been an absolute failure of a husband, in so many of the ways that mattered. True, he'd provided financially, more than Isabella could ever want. And their sex life had been decent, when he was home to be with her. But the time she'd craved, the emotional intimacy, he'd withheld—without intending to—because his focus had been so completely on his fast-growing empire.

By the time he returned to the cabin, Genevieve was dressed in the same clothes she'd been wearing that first day, and her hair had been styled into a neat ponytail. She looked so untouchable and sophisticated, so he craved to drop to his knees and remind her of the wildness that ran through her. To make her scream his name, one last time.

But something had shifted between them, with the discovery of the photograph. Her eyes wouldn't quite hold his and her smile, once glorious and glowing, was now brittle like an aged animal bone.

'Is the boat on the way?'

He nodded towards the window. 'It's almost here.'

He didn't look at her to see the reaction.

'Great. I should set off, then.'

'There is another path to the beach,' he said. 'I'll show you.'

'No need.' That same brittle tone permeated her voice. 'If you just point me in the direction, I'll be fine.'

'I don't want your death on my conscience, remember?'

She flinched at that and he made an effort to soften his tone. But he didn't feel soft. He felt the very opposite of it. Anger with his life, his choices, with everything, twisted inside him.

'I will not argue about this,' he said flatly. 'Are you ready?'

Her skin was pale but she held her ground. 'Of course. I can't wait to leave.' She stalked towards the door but then paused, and looked around, as if she wanted to remember it. When her eyes landed on the bookshelf, they narrowed, and her spine straightened with renewed determination. She spun away from him and stepped out into the winter sunshine.

He told himself he was glad to see the back of her.

The whole walk down to the beach—much more easily accomplished through this path, which was wide enough for a car, and had probably been used to bring supplies for the cabin, when it was being built—she fumed. She couldn't believe this was how it was ending between them.

Why hadn't he told her about his wife? And even then, when she'd found the photo, why hadn't he just given her a rundown of what had happened?

It was James all over again. A man she'd given herself to who'd kept the important pieces of himself locked away.

She ground her teeth to stop from crying, but inside, years of grief and pain were folding around this new rejection and hurt, so she felt physically weakened by everything she'd been through. And this was supposed to have been the start of the new phase of her life. Her pleasure. Her redemption arc.

A single tear rolled down one cheek and she was grateful Nikos was walking to her other side, so she could surreptitiously wipe it away as she turned to look at the stunning view. Now she could see other islands in the distance, and possibly even the mainland. So they had not been so isolated, after all.

The ocean was so deceptively calm now. It was hard to imagine the swell that had tipped her boat clean over, snapping the mast in half.

The ground began to level off, and compressed gravel gave way to sand, down the far end of the cove she'd landed in. If she'd kept walking, she would have eventually found this clearing and been able to walk a much easier path to the cabin, she thought derisively. But the weather had been so bad, she had hardly been able to see five feet in front of herself, much less to the end of the beach.

A small rubber dinghy had been brought right onto the sand. She eyed it simply to avoid looking at Nikos.

'Genevieve,' he said, voice deep. She closed her eyes, stomach clenching.

She turned to face him then, waiting, aware that there was a man standing with the rubber dinghy who was also waiting.

'It's fine,' she said, when it really wasn't. But her marriage to James had taught her to hide her pain and process it later. It was her conditioning, and in that moment she was glad for it.

He stared at her, long and hard.

'This was just sex,' she reminded him, pleased her tone sounded light. 'It was great. Fun. But we always knew I'd leave when I could. So…thanks.'

'Thanks,' he repeated, his brows quirking.

She nodded, knowing she needed to leave, but finding her feet strangely recalcitrant. 'Thanks,' she said again. 'And good luck. With the island and everything.' It made no sense. She was babbling. 'Okay. Bye.'

She turned to walk away from him, plastering a smile on her face as she approached the waiting man, who, to her relief, spoke English, so she was saved the further need of involving Nikos. She gave the name of the town she was staying in, and then went to climb into the dinghy. But Nikos was suddenly there, and her heart went into overdrive with an emotion she'd thought she'd learned to suppress: hope.

He was not there to ask her to stay though. Nor to apologise for keeping something so important secret. He simply held out his hand and offered it to her, to steady her as she stepped into the small rubber boat. She thought about not taking it. She thought about ignoring him. But then, the boat rocked a little and the thought of falling into the ocean at his feet had her weakening, and placing her hand in his, to step onto the craft. Sparks exploded beneath her skin as her body, used now to craving him at the slightest touch, burst with anticipation.

She tried to tamp down on those feelings: she'd never know the pleasure of Nikos's possession again. And though the storm had cleared, as the man began to row the dinghy towards the large speedboat, she felt as though a dark cloud had appeared, right over her.

She didn't look back, and he was glad. But for his part, Nikos stayed on the beach, watching the boat, until it had turned into a tiny white dot on the horizon. And the whole time, he told himself he'd done the right thing. He clung to that, until he reached the cabin and saw small signs of her occupancy everywhere. From the neatly made bed—she must have done that while he called Theo then stayed out of the cabin—to the two cups and two plates that were still drying on the edge of the bench from the night before. She was in the Irish strawberries that were in the middle of the table, a pretty arrangement she'd made with the few he'd stuffed into his pockets during the break in the storm. And she was in the bookshelf—the way the cookbook had been placed differently, in haste, by his own hand, made him realise he hadn't pulled it out to look at it in over a year.

He moved to it now and opened it to the page with the photograph, closing his eyes a moment against the swell of pain that predictably enveloped him.

He pressed a finger to Isabella, guilt and grief mixing to push everything else from his mind. 'I'm so sorry,' he said, but he could no longer be sure if he was talking about Isabella or Genevieve.

For the first time in a long time, he dreamed of Isabella. It was a little like a memory, yet it was different from what had actually happened. She looked different. Her hair was short and her eyes were blue. *Why won't you fight with me? Why won't you shout and yell?* He'd never shouted. Why would he? She'd never made him angry, she'd never made him anything other than frustrated, and even then, he'd simply wanted her to be happy. *You keep so much of yourself locked up. I hate it! Don't you think I deserve the respect of honesty, at least? Don't you think I deserve that, Nikos?*

She'd said that often. She'd worried he was cheating, when, of course, he never would. He had simply worked long hours. But to Isabella, honesty had been the hallmark of a good relationship. It had been everything to her. Which was why she'd told him when she'd slept with another man. Only she'd told him in that way of wanting to hurt him, of hoping it might mean he would show something more to her. That it might snap him out of his obsessive work fog. It hadn't. He'd asked if she wanted a divorce, and she'd sobbed, shaken her head, and fallen into his arms. He'd forgiven her easily. It was Isabella; he'd wanted her to be happy.

She deserves the truth, too. Don't be like her husband. Don't hurt when you can heal.

The words were in his dream, but they might as well have been a sledgehammer against his temple, for how they acted to wake him up. He pushed up in the bed and stared at the wall opposite, his mind spinning over that, his breath coming in rushed fits and spurts.

He hadn't wanted to hurt Genevieve. His own pain was something he relished, something he sought at every opportunity. But Genevieve, he'd wanted to help. To heal, just as Isabella, in his dreams, had said.

The thought of Genevieve being back in Katanos, being hurt that he didn't tell her about Isabella, thinking that it was in some way a reflection of her, rather than it being who *he* was, and he knew he couldn't leave things as they were. He'd had three long years to carry his guilt. There was nothing he could do for Isabella now, except suffer because of how he'd treated her. But at least he could explain to Genevieve. It was the very least he owed her.

CHAPTER EIGHT

KATANOS WAS A small coastal town, and though it was very beautiful, it was not really set up to cater for tourists. In summer, she could imagine it might be busier, but now, in winter, the place was quiet, populated sparsely with locals. She'd had her choice of the two hotels, and had opted for the smaller, because it had sweeping views out over the water. Now, however, she couldn't look towards the windows without thinking of Nikos. In the distance, she was sure she could make out the cliff faces of his island, the dense forest that covered them, and any time she happened to glance in that direction, she felt a pounding of blood in her ears.

An anger and hurt, a twisting inside her to know she'd never see him again. It was what they'd agreed to, and she'd known it all along, but, despite her best efforts, he'd got under her skin.

She'd become used to him.

She'd allowed herself to like him. Maybe, in the very back of her mind, even to want *more* from him. How stupid was she? After everything she'd been through with James, she should have been giving all men a seriously wide berth. Not falling into bed with the first willing partner.

Then again, she'd never regret that.

If nothing else, Nikos had given Genevieve the first orgasms of her life. He'd shown her something vital and true about herself, that she'd always doubted—that she was a sexual woman, after all, capable of enjoying that act, of feeling intense pleasure. The problem hadn't been with her. Maybe it hadn't even been with James, so much as their shared chemistry. They just weren't compatible, on so many levels.

Unlike her and Nikos.

She sucked in a sharp breath as the pain of that lanced through her. It was almost impossible to believe she wouldn't see him again.

All night, she'd been disoriented. She'd drifted off to sleep, only to reach for Nikos, looking for the warmth of his huge body, for the pleasure of his touch, only to wake and remember his rejection, his cold acceptance of her leaving the island.

Finally, at dawn, she'd given up on trying to sleep and had slipped out of bed, pulled on a maxi dress and denim jacket, some dark sunglasses, and set off on a long walk, in the hope that, with exertion, she might be able to finally put him from her mind, once and for all.

Katanos was not a large town, and with only two hotels, and the influence of who he was, it took Nikos no time whatsoever to ascertain at which hotel Genevieve was a guest. It took even less time to establish that she'd left that morning, and not yet returned. Unused to waiting, and not enjoying the way locals stared at him in the foyer, he nonetheless settled himself in one of the chairs so he would see when she returned.

Discomfort was his constant companion, though. He was aware of the way people looked at him. His wealth had made him well known, but his reclusiveness made him famous. He'd dealt with this before. Any time he showed his face in Athens, he was treated like some kind of god.

He didn't once consider leaving though. Having decided to speak to Genevieve, he had no intention of failing. Not again. And so, he waited, eyes trained on the door, ignoring the way every man and his dog stopped and stared, unable to believe that they'd seen The Nikos Konstantinou, with their own eyes.

She walked far longer and further than she'd intended, so it was after lunch by the time Genevieve made her way back to the hotel, thinking of the half-eaten sandwich in her small mini bar with a sudden pang of hunger. She had barely eaten since leaving the island, and now felt a little light-headed.

She was distracted as she approached the hotel, so didn't notice the couple standing at the windows, peering inside. Even if she had, she would have presumed they were simply admiring the mid-century décor, or something equally banal.

But when she pushed in the door and her eyes glanced across the lobby, she saw him immediately. How could she not? On the island, there'd been something fitting about his size, his animalistic wildness. But here—even when dressed in dark trousers and a business shirt—he looked like a wolf in sheep's clothing. Quite literally. She stopped walking, almost unable to believe he was here. Unable to believe that she hadn't conjured him up out of thin air. But then, of their own volition, her feet began to move, carrying her towards him, as he stood and started to stride over the orange carpet.

But as they walked towards one another, something was dinging in the back of her mind. A distant alarm. On the island, he'd been so elemental and raw, as if formed from the clay of the cliffs, the wildness of the ocean. Here, in these clothes, there was something almost familiar about him. She frowned, dispelling the thought. *Of course* he was familiar. They'd spent days becoming intimately acquainted.

'You really do have a death wish,' he muttered.

She startled, staring up at him. The sensible question of 'what are you doing here?' was usurped by, 'What's that supposed to mean?'

'One minute you are gallivanting around on a tiny sailboat in a wild storm, the next you are walking in the middle of the day, without a hat?'

'It's winter.'

'It is warm and your cheeks are flushed. Are you burned?'

She stared at him as though he'd lost his mind. Could he really not work out why her cheeks were pink?

'I'm fine,' she said through gritted teeth, taking a step back, and wobbling a little—from surprise at seeing him again. His hand swooped out immediately, before she'd even registered her reaction, and curled around her back, drawing her against his body. Which really, really didn't help matters at all.

'You look like you are about to pass out,' he muttered, condemnation in the words.

'I'm not,' she denied, though, in truth, she did feel very weak all of a sudden. 'I'm just hungry. I haven't eaten yet.'

He looked as though he wanted to snap at that, and inwardly, she dared him to. She was fed up with this man—blowing hot, cold, and right back into her life when she'd spent the last thirty hours forcing herself to accept the brutal reality of never seeing him again.

'Then let's go and eat.'

She opened her mouth to tell him, witheringly, that she had a sandwich in her room, but as she mentally conjured an image of that small space, with its double bed in the centre, she clamped her lips together. Better to avoid being in a hotel room with this man right now. She might have been annoyed with him, but there was no way she could deny the effect his proximity was having on her pulse.

'Why are you here?' she asked, instead.

'We need to talk.'

She shook her head. 'Not as far as I'm concerned.'

'I owe you an explanation,' he said, still holding her against his body. 'You were right: I should have told you about her.'

Genevieve's eyes swept shut on a wave of surprise. Nikos was clearly different from James in myriad ways, but this was yet another. James *never* admitted to having made a mistake, and he never apologised for anything. He certainly never explained his actions. Nikos's willingness to do so brought a heady rush of power to her brain, and a strangely heartening sense of security. It threatened to undermine all her sense and reason, her rational thoughts. Because regardless of his good points, he was still a man, still someone she needed to treat with caution. Not because of him, but because of herself, her battered heart, her destroyed abilities to trust.

'Yes, you should have,' she said, making a half-hearted effort to push away from him. But he held her up regardless, his arm like a vice around her waist, offering support that, in fact, she did feel she needed.

'Then let me tell you now.'

'Fine. Tell me.' She tilted her face to his defiantly, but his eyes shifted over her shoulder, towards the door. She turned to look in that direction to see a middle-aged couple walking down the street.

'Can we go to your room?'

'No way, buster. Tell me this isn't some kind of inter-island booty call.'

'It's not,' he muttered.

'Tell me here.'

'No.' He looked around, then let out a rough breath. 'Come with me.'

She shook her head. 'Not until you tell me where we're going.'

'For lunch. You need to eat, and I would prefer not to have this conversation in the middle of a hotel foyer.' His eyes bored into hers, as grey as the stormy ocean, and she lost herself for a moment in their depths. She thought she might actually agree to anything he asked of her, if she wasn't careful.

'Fine. I know a place nearby.'

She could see that he didn't like that. Nikos, she suspected, was very used to calling the shots. But Genevieve had been in a relationship like that, and it had nearly been the death of her. She arched a single brow, silently challenging him to argue, but he didn't.

'Fine. I presume it's close?'

'Just next door.'

'Show me.' He kept his arm around her waist as they walked from the hotel, offering her support. She wasn't sure she needed it now the shock of seeing him had passed, but she didn't say as much to him. Not when it felt so good to be held close to his large, strong body. Besides, what was the harm? They were on the other side of the world from Washington—thousands of miles from her ex-husband's sphere of influence. He would never find out about this.

The waiter who'd led them to a table was little more than a child, fourteen or fifteen at most, and he'd shown more interest in his mobile phone than he had in his guests, so for once, Nikos wasn't recognised when he arrived at a restaurant. Thank *Christos*, because the last thing he needed was for this to go out of order.

The more he'd thought about it, the more he'd realised how much of himself he'd kept locked away from Genevieve. Strangely, though, he'd told her many of the most important details of who he was. Away from the glitz and wealth of his success, he'd told her about his father and his upbringing, his values and his life on the island. To say she didn't know him wouldn't be accurate.

Not entirely.

They were seated at a table in the back of the restaurant, and Nikos chose to face the wall, ostensibly to give Genevieve a better view. It had the added advantage of giving him a greater chance of not being recognised.

As they sat down, he ordered pitta bread and dips, and a bottle of local wine, before turning his attention on Genevieve. She was regarding him with an air of mistrust. He couldn't blame her. Not after what she'd been through with her ex-husband, particularly.

'So?' she prompted, toying with the napkin in the same way she had his sheets, reminding him suddenly of bed, with her, and the way their limbs had tangled as they'd made love, each as frantic as the other to be together, as though their lives depended on it.

He looked away quickly, swallowing, trying to control his body's immediate reaction to that thought.

'You were going to tell me about your wife?' Genevieve said, voice slightly rushed.

He jerked his gaze to hers, nodding. 'Yes. Isabella,' he said, clearing his throat afterwards. He hadn't mentioned her name to anyone besides his father-in-law in a long time.

'You're divorced?' Genevieve prompted.

The waiter appeared then, placing the bottle of wine down, removing the cork, which he shoved into his apron pocket at the same time he removed his phone.

Nikos poured two glasses then sat back in his chair.

'Well?' Genevieve asked impatiently as she reached for her wine and took a sip.

'I'm not divorced, no.'

All the colour drained from her face. 'Nikos.' His name was a plea. At first, he presumed she'd intuited what he was struggling to say, but then he connected the dots and remembered what her loser ex had put her through, with his affairs. 'I can't—' she whispered, taking another huge sip of wine before standing up and looking around desperately, then stepping away from her seat, as if to leave the restaurant.

He reached out quickly, put a hand on her wrist, holding her where she was. Her eyes flooded with tears and, God help him, the sight of her about to cry brought back so many memories of Isabella, he felt the bottom fall out of his world.

'She's dead,' he said, the words catching in his throat. He hated to acknowledge that reality, let alone admit it to someone else. 'My wife died, Genevieve.'

A single tear slid down her cheek as she stared at him, so close her leg brushed his thigh. 'I—she died?'

He dropped her wrist and stared straight ahead. 'A little over three years ago.'

He heard her move seconds before she took the seat opposite him again. But she reached out and covered his hand with hers, all soft compassion in the lines of her eyes. 'And you moved to the island.'

'I didn't move to the island,' he muttered, figuring he might as well give her the whole, ugly truth now. 'I bought it fully intending that it would kill me.'

She gasped.

'I deserved to die, Genevieve. I deserved to know the same pain and loneliness she had known. You and my late wife have something in common, you see.'

Genevieve was silent, staring across at him.

'You were both married to bastards.'

She shook her head, instantly rejecting his statement. 'Don't say that.'

'I ruined her life,' he said, the words pouring out of him now, so he barely noticed when the waiter appeared, depositing bread and dips. 'I took someone beautiful, something beautiful, and destroyed it. And she told me.

She told me again and again how miserable she was, how unhappy. I could have changed; I just chose not to.'

'I don't understand,' Genevieve said, shaking her head. 'You're not cruel, Nikos. How can you blame yourself for this? What did you do to make her miserable?'

'I married her, knowing she loved me with her dying breath. Knowing I was the sun and moon of her existence. I married her knowing that I would probably never feel that about her. And then I ignored her, focusing instead on my work. All I cared about was financial success. Proving myself to the world, her father, my father, may he rest in peace, to the men who took advantage of my mother, to anyone who'd ever doubted me. Isabella was left married to a man who loved her as an abstract concept, an object, rather than through his actions. She deserved so much better.'

Genevieve closed her eyes and he was glad. He couldn't bear the sympathy he'd seen in their depths. It was everything he'd hidden away from, that he knew he didn't deserve.

'Nikos,' she whispered, when she blinked and looked across at him again. 'You cannot carry this burden.'

He stiffened, pulling his hand away from her. 'I didn't tell you because I wanted sympathy. Nor because I wanted you to make me feel better. In fact, that's the opposite of what I want. I intend to spend the rest of my life deep in this regret.'

'Hiding away on your island?' she asked, sipping her wine, her voice neutral and yet still, somehow, scathing.

'You have a problem with that?'

'Well, what good does it do anyone?'

'I'm not seeking to do anyone anything.'

'You're seeking to punish yourself.'

He stared back at her, unable and unwilling to dispute that.

'To what end?'

'I'm sorry?'

She compressed her lips. 'What does it achieve?'

'It is less about what it achieves, and more about what I deserve.'

'Fine. You say Isabella loved you with her whole heart. Do you think *she* would want this for you?'

He felt a muscle tic in his jaw at the sensible question. It wasn't the first time it had been said to him. His father-in-law had implored him not to throw his life away in Isabella's name. But it was what Nikos deserved.

'Honestly, I think you're doing her a huge injustice.'

He made a sound of surprise. 'I beg your pardon?'

'I was in a deeply unhappy marriage. I was young and naïve when I met James, and I let him sweep me up utterly and completely into all that he promised. But it was a terrible mistake. You know what I did?'

Nikos reached for his own wine then, taking a sip, before he replaced it on the table and took a triangle of bread, spreading it generously with taramasalata then putting it on Genevieve's plate.

'Eat,' he said, not even trying to keep the tone of command from his voice.

She glared at him. 'Do you know what I did?'

He looked pointedly at the bread so with a dramatic huff she lifted it to her mouth and took a bite. And despite the tenor of their conversation, his eyes clung to her mouth, her sweet pink lips, as she chewed and swallowed. He looked away abruptly, barely able to focus on what they'd been discussing.

'I left him,' she said, eventually. 'It was hard, and I had to basically sign my life away to get out, but I did it. Because I realised I couldn't live the rest of my days like that. So unless there was something you were holding over Isabella's head, making it impossible for her to leave, unless you were making promises you had no intention of keeping, then I think you can safely assume she stayed because no matter what, she wanted to. Because she loved you.'

'Yes, she loved me,' he spat. 'But I made her miserable. Loving me ruined her life. *I* should have left *her*.'

'You don't think that would have ruined her life, too?'

'Then I should never have married her.'

'Perhaps, but you did. I can only presume you loved her, as well.'

He stopped then, dropping his gaze to his plate as he thought of Isabella as she'd been then. When they'd both been young and carefree. 'Yes,' he said, simply. 'I loved her, but not how she loved me. Not enough. I did want to make her happy. It just turned out that there were other things I wanted more.'

Genevieve's sympathetic expression had his gut turning.

'Please, don't pity me.'

'Why not?'

'Because I don't want it, least of all from you.'

'I feel like there's an insult in there.'

'I don't deserve it from you.'

'Please don't let me become something else you beat yourself up about,' she said, shaking her head. 'You didn't do anything wrong, Nikos. Even not telling me about Isabella was your prerogative. We were clear about the nature of our relationship from the outset. Just because I opened up to you didn't obligate you to do the same to me.'

'You were upset.'

'Yes, I was, but both things can be true at once.'

He quirked a brow.

'I was upset you hadn't told me about Isabella, but at the same time, it wasn't your fault. It's just…one of those things.'

'When you told me about your husband, and how selfish he was, all I could think was that I could give you something special. Something joyous. When you told me he'd never given you pleasure, I ached to offer that to you.'

'And you did,' she said, before her eyes widened and then blinked away. 'Because of her,' Genevieve said. 'It was never really about me, was it?'

He frowned, trying to work back what he'd said.

'You are so torn apart by what you perceive you failed to give your wife that you thought you could make some sort of amends with me. Right?'

He found it hard to draw breath. He thought about denying it, but why? She was right. He had sought penance, in Genevieve. 'Two birds, one stone.'

She let out a low whistle and then glanced over his shoulder.

'Do you know those people?'

He braced himself even as he turned around, to see a group of women by the counter all looking at him. When he turned their way, one of them snapped a photo. He grimaced as he spun back to Genevieve.

'No.'

'They seem to know you.'

He dipped his head in silent acknowledgement.

Genevieve's voice was a little uneven when she spoke next, her eyes widening. He could practically see the penny dropping. Slowly, but dropping nonetheless. 'But you grew up around here, so they must know you, or your parents…'

'They know of me, not me personally.'

Genevieve sat a little straighter, voice strained. 'Why would they know of you?'

'Because I'm Nikos Konstantinou and in Greece, at least, that makes me famous.'

CHAPTER NINE

'NOT JUST IN GREECE,' she said, voice shaking, looking around with a sinking feeling of absolute desperation. And though Genevieve rarely drank alcohol, she reached for the wine and finished her glass, panic setting her nerves on edge. 'You're famous everywhere. Nikos. Oh my God. You're Nikos Konstantinou. You are...very famous,' she hissed. 'How could you not tell me this?' But how had she not put two and two together? True, he looked very different from any mental image she had of the man—and even then, it wasn't as though she had a clear image. It was his *name* that was synonymous with success and wealth, his *name* that was spoken in all the business circles.

He grimaced. 'Does it matter?'

'Not on the island, no, and not to me. I don't care *who* you are. But those people were taking photos of you. Of *us*. If they end up on the Internet, or on gossip sites—'

'They will,' he muttered, tone frustrated. 'The flipside of living a reclusive life is that when I show my face anywhere, it makes the news.'

'The news,' she exclaimed, looking around urgently. 'I need to get out of here. At least this doesn't look too bad. I can explain having lunch with you,' she rambled, reaching into her handbag and pulling out some money, placing it on the table between them as she stood. 'No one needs to know— Oh, God. But the lobby. You had your arm around me for minutes. Someone probably saw, and took photos there, right?'

He nodded once.

'Oh Nikos,' she groaned, dropping her head into her hands. 'I have to get out of here,' she repeated, looking around. Nikos was standing then, ignoring the cash she'd left on the table. He reached down and took her hand.

'No,' she said, quickly pulling her own away. 'Don't touch me. That's just going to make this so much worse.'

'Let's go to your hotel.'

This time, she didn't argue. At least that was private, and, God knew, sex was the last thing on her mind in that moment. 'Fine,' she said, through gritted teeth. 'Just don't touch me. I need to think.'

She'd never been so grateful in her life than that she'd suggested a restaurant right next door to her hotel. It was easy to pick their way across the cobblestoned footpath towards the lobby. Now, though, that the shock of seeing Nikos had worn off, she was aware of how many people were looking in their direction. Her stomach was in loops as they rode the elevator side by side, for Genevieve's part being careful not to so much as brush her hand against his.

The doors opened into a blessedly deserted corridor, with the same mid-century décor—brown and orange accent colours and yellow light shades. She slid the key into the door, twisted it then stepped inside, holding it open for Nikos to pass. Until he stepped into the room, she hadn't even noticed how narrow the little entrance way was, but it was physically impossible for him to pass by the door when she was standing there without brushing against her. A fact her body rejoiced in even as her mind was trying to calm things down.

He moved beyond her, thank goodness, into the room, allowing her a moment to take in a breath as she shut the door behind them.

'You're Nikos Konstantinou,' she muttered, crossing her arms over her chest as she raked her gaze across the man in front of her.

Not only was the entrance corridor tiny, but the room seemed it now, too. He looked around, as if at a loss for where to stand, and eventually settled for moving towards the window. His gaze shifted to the view, and she wondered if he was doing what she had so often in the last twenty-four hours: looking for the island.

'It's not relevant.'

She compressed her lips.

'Nikos, this is a disaster.'

He angled his face to hers. 'That might be the first time any woman has ever had that reaction.'

She ignored his arrogant response. 'If you're trying to be funny, quit it. This is not amusing.'

His eyes bored into hers. 'Do I look amused?'

'Nikos, I have…an agreement with my ex-husband. I can't be photographed with you. I can't have those photos hit the Internet.' Her skin felt all cold and clammy, and she must have looked awful because a moment later he was sweeping across the room and drawing her to the bed.

'Sit,' he commanded, and then eased her down when she didn't immediately comply. He crouched in front of her, reminding Genevieve of that first evening in the cabin, when he'd patched up her wounds so tenderly. 'Tell me about this agreement.'

Now that she knew who he was, she could see the easy command with which he approached situations. It had been obvious on the island, but she'd put that down to his superior outdoor skills. Now, she saw it for what it was, as she was in possession of all the facts: this man was a born leader. A dynamic, brilliant, world-leading entrepreneur, who was worth more money than she could even contemplate.

If James saw photographs of her and Nikos together, he'd lose it. He'd renege on their agreement, and use her breach as the cause. He'd stop paying the medical bills. He'd go to the press with the truth of her father's gambling, ruining his reputation. She felt herself trembling and clasped her hands together in an attempt to stop it.

'Start at the beginning,' he suggested.

She couldn't really imagine saying 'no' to Nikos. Not when he was in this mode. 'Our divorce was not amicable,' she said slowly. 'He didn't want me to leave, but I threatened to go to the press if he made me stay. It was…a tense negotiation,' she whispered. 'To put it mildly.'

Nikos's face was blanked of emotion, but she knew him too well. Those eyes of his, stormy like the sea, gave away his distaste.

'Our prenuptial agreement was ironclad. I wasn't entitled to anything, besides a very small stipend. My mother's medical bills are insane, and James is paying them. I didn't have a job—James didn't want me to work, and I agreed, at first, because I thought I was in love, and then, because I was so desperate to keep the peace…'

Nikos nodded, silently encouraging her to continue,

but Genevieve was in the past, reliving that godawful day when they'd sat across a long table in his lawyers' offices and worked through the details.

And then, the moment he'd had the lawyers leave, to show just how completely he wanted to ruin her life.

She sucked in a deep breath.

'He agreed to pay off the bills, on two conditions. The first, that I sign a non-disclosure agreement about our marriage. I'm not supposed to have even told you what I did. And if I'd known who you are, and the circles you have access to,' she said, dropping her head forward. 'You and James probably know several of the same people.'

'I have no intention of betraying a word you've told me.'

Even without him saying that, she knew it to be true. She didn't really want to think about the trust she felt for him—it ran counter to every pledge she'd made herself, post-divorce.

'I just thought—'

'That I was a cave dweller,' he supplied, his hand moving to her thigh and rubbing there.

She squeezed her eyes shut. 'I thought you were as far removed from that whole world as anyone.'

'I am.'

She shook her head. 'You're really not.'

'What was his second requirement?'

'I'm not allowed to date anyone. I'm not allowed to "disgrace" or "humiliate" him by moving on before he's ready for me to. His political career is too important to him, and he wants to manage the optics of this,' she said, shaking her head. Hating that, on some level, she understood that. When she glanced at Nikos, she was reminded of the thunderclouds over his island on the day she'd crashed to the shore.

'I see,' he drawled, sounding as though he wanted to punch something.

'I can't...if he sees those photographs, he's going to stop paying those bills, and I can't afford...'

'I'll pay them.'

She blanched, feeling physically ill at the suggestion. 'Absolutely not.' She jackknifed off the bed, somehow managing to sidestep him in her desperation to get away. 'No way.'

'You know I have the money.'

She whirled around to the windows. 'That's not the point.'

'Are you sure?'

'I will *never* make the mistake of being beholden to another man. I will not owe you that.'

'I will pay it as a gift.'

'No!' she shouted, then spun back to face him. 'No.'

'Isn't it better than having him pay the money?'

'He owes me,' she snapped. 'After what he put me through, I have no conscience issues with him paying for my mother's medical expenses. If I'd had a better lawyer before we got married, I would have been entitled to far more in our prenup. But—' She lifted a hand, to silence whatever he'd been about to say. 'I am keeping a tab of everything he's spent, since our divorce, and I intend to pay him back, when I can afford to.'

Nikos's expression grew more thunderous by the second. 'So you would rather let that low-life pay, than me?'

'This isn't about you,' she said, shaking her head. 'I

mean, it is. But your money isn't relevant to me. Besides, there's more at stake.'

He crossed his arms over his broad chest, staring her down.

'Early on in our marriage, before I knew what he was like, I told him about my father. His gambling. James has made it abundantly clear that if I don't abide by the terms of our agreement, he'll go to the press with a tell-all story.'

'Who would care?'

'My father,' she whispered.

'Your father is dead.'

'Yes, but his legacy, his family's legacy…it means something. I loved him, Nikos.' She bit back a sob. 'I can't let this be what he's remembered for.'

Nikos's jaw moved as he ground his teeth together.

'This is a disaster,' she said, shaking her head. 'I should never have let this happen. You should never have come here.'

'I had no way of knowing you had entered into this deal with your ex-husband.'

'No, but…' She tapered off, struck by the fairness of his words. She moved back to the edge of the bed and sat down again, dropping her head into her hands. 'He's going to be so angry.'

'Yes,' Nikos said, moving to stand in front of her. 'He sounds like the kind of prick whose tiny ego would be wounded by this.'

She almost smiled at the description but, in truth, her insides were in too much turmoil.

'Nikos,' she groaned. 'You need to leave. If any of the hotel staff saw you come in here and decide to make a quick buck, it's just going to go from bad to worse. I might be able to explain away the lunch…'

'But not the lobby,' he reminded her grimly.

She closed her eyes, remembering the way they'd seemingly embraced for minutes, bodies melded together in an undeniably intimate fashion.

'No,' she whispered.

'Then you can't cross your fingers and hope he won't find out. He'll see the photos.'

She worried her lower lip between her teeth, anxiety spiralling through her.

'The world will see the photos, and your name will be linked to his. It's impossible to avoid, I'm afraid.'

Her gut rolled, because he was right.

'You have two options, Genevieve.'

'Really? I feel like I have zero options.'

He crouched down in front of her. 'Don't do that.'

She blinked at him.

'Don't give up. You survived being capsized during a brutal storm then hiked for miles in the pouring rain, scaling cliff faces in a dark, unfamiliar forest. Not to mention two nights in a cabin with me. You are a fighter. Don't let that piece of shit make you forget it.'

Her heart twisted at that. His words, and his vision of her. It was so warming, so uplifting, she found herself almost forgetting the nightmare of her situation, simply so she could revel in the way he saw her.

'The cabin with you was really no hardship,' she felt compelled to say.

He squeezed her legs. 'Either you face up to him, and suffer the consequences. On your own, if you insist,' he said, before she could argue. 'Or you let me help you.'

Her heart twisted as she shook her head. 'I can't, Nikos. We barely know each other.'

His expression darkened. 'That is not how I would characterise our relationship.'

'That's because you're a hermit,' she muttered. 'And help me how? I don't want your money.'

'I will *loan* you the money,' he said. 'And you can pay me back whenever you're ready. I cannot see it's any worse than owing him.'

She shook her head. How could she make him understand? She didn't want to owe anyone anything. 'Even if you did, he'd still go to the press about Dad. Don't you get it? He's got me over a barrel. He always did.'

A muscle ticced in his jaw. 'Yes,' he said, after a beat. 'Which is why we'll get engaged.'

If she'd been drinking, she would have spat it out. She spluttered her surprise, coughing because then she lost her breath.

'I am *not* marrying you. Or anyone. Ever. No way.'

'I have no intention of getting married either.'

She blinked at him through the tears her shortness of breath had produced. 'I don't understand.'

'Being engaged is not the same thing as getting married. We'll enter into a fake engagement, so your husband knows that if he messes with you, he gets me, too.'

She stared at him with total shock. It was not, in fact, the worst plan she'd heard. Knowing James, the misogynistic jackass, as she did, only the presence of someone bigger, stronger and richer would ever have a chance in hell of cowering him. While she absolutely despised the reality of that, she knew it to be the case. If she took option A, and confronted him alone, she had no doubt James would let all hell break loose. Including humiliating her father's memory, for the sake of it.

But with Nikos apparently in her life and by her side, she doubted James would be stupid enough to do anything.

'I can't ask you to do that,' she said, shaking her head, even as the possibility spread through her.

'You are not asking. I am suggesting it. If I thought it appropriate, I would insist upon it, but it would be better for both of us if you came to the decision yourself.'

She narrowed her eyes at that, ignoring the feeling she might be getting out of the frying pan and into the fire, moving from one dictatorial man to another. Nikos was *not* like James. He was commanding and in control, but he was also respectful and fair.

Hadn't she thought the same thing about James though, at first? Hadn't she believed him to be all that was good and decent?

What if she was wrong about Nikos? She needed an insurance policy, something to protect her. 'This could be a very bad idea.'

'Why?'

'Honestly? Because I'm scared. I'm scared of letting my guard down, especially with someone like you.'

'That makes sense. You don't want to get hurt again.'

She nodded.

'Will it placate you if I promise that, from this point on, I will do everything in my power to ensure that doesn't happen?'

She pulled her lips to the side. 'I don't know.'

'This does not need to last long. A few weeks of being photographed together, and, at some point, the inevitable confrontation with your ex, and then we can quietly go back to our normal lives. If he approaches you, you can contact me through my business manager, Theo, and I will reappear, to make sure he doesn't step out of line.'

It was tempting. Tempting because the idea of having someone like Nikos to throw in James's face made her battered and bruised heart lift with pleasure.

But this was Nikos's life. 'Surely this is your worst nightmare.'

He stood then, looking down at her with a set jaw. 'I could not help my mother. I didn't help my wife. Let me at least help you.'

Her heart then, already ripped to shreds by everything she'd been through, felt newly damaged by Nikos's admission, and how he viewed himself.

'Oh, Nikos,' she murmured, shaking her head. 'I can't use your guilt like that.'

'I will feel it, no matter what. At least this way, I have an option to make amends. Let me help, Genevieve. I'm begging you.'

As the words had formed on his lips, and he'd heard them in the room, he'd wanted to suck them right back in again. A fake engagement? And everything that meant? The idea of reappearing on the Athens society circuit, engaged to someone else? So Isabella would be relegated to a figment of his past. Worse, willingly creating the impression that he'd moved on from Isabella?

But the more he looked at Genevieve, and saw her desperate, stressed features, and thought of the man responsible for that, he knew he had to act as a shield for her. To protect her in a way he desperately wished someone had protected Isabella, or his mother.

More than that, he knew Isabella would want him to do this. She would be the first to counsel him to care for someone in need, to give of himself.

So when Genevieve looked up at him and nodded her agreement, albeit with a look of swirling doubt in her eyes, he knew for certain this was the right choice. Which was not the same thing as looking forward to it. All he wanted was to turn tail and run back to his island, to his solitude and cabin, to the life he'd had before Genevieve. And yet, strangely, he wanted to drag Genevieve back there with him, too.

CHAPTER TEN

THE TRANSITION FROM mountain man to billionaire—albeit rugged, enormous billionaire—happened far quicker than Genevieve wanted. When Nikos returned to her hotel room that evening, he'd shaved his island stubble, had his hair trimmed, and he wore a suit. The kind of suit she'd sworn she couldn't imagine him in, because he'd been so at home in casual clothes. Or nothing at all.

Now, though, he wore something that looked custom-made. Well, it would probably have to be, given his proportions. Proportions that fairly engulfed her as they left the hotel and slipped into his waiting car. A man with dark hair was behind the wheel and he said something obviously deferential when they slid into the back seat—going by the tone, rather than the language, which was Greek.

'I don't know if I'll get used to you like this,' Genevieve said, a little breathily, as the car took off from the hotel.

He slid her a look that showed he felt the same, and, with her stomach in knots, they drove the rest of the way in silence. It wasn't far, though. Perhaps ten minutes later, the car slid through a set of open gates then stopped, and when Genevieve looked out, she saw a gleaming black helicopter with a golden 'K' on the tail.

K for Konstantinou.

She fell into step beside him as he opened a hinged door and then held out his hand to help her up into the helicopter. She glanced at him a little nervously. 'Do I need to lift you?'

'I've only been in a helicopter once. I didn't enjoy it.'

'Do you want to drive instead?'

She looked at him and shook her head, forcing herself to be brave. This was the second phase of her life; she was no longer going to be shaped by fear. And in part, that was because Nikos was helping her grow beyond that. She couldn't run and hide from James for ever; she had to face her demons, to face him.

'No, it's okay,' she said, with renewed determination, as she put one foot on the ledge then swung herself into the supple leather seat. Nikos shut the door firmly then came around to the front pilot side, opening the door and swinging his frame in, before reaching across and threading her arms through the seat belts. Something she definitely could have done if she'd been a little less preoccupied by the whole helicopter thing.

It was when his eyes hooked to hers though, and his hand went between her legs, to retrieve the buckle, that she gasped audibly, gaze falling on him in a way they both understood. No matter what had happened since, no matter how complex this arrangement had the potential to be, this part was simple. He touched her, and her body reacted. And vice versa. She could see it in the way his hand lingered against her sex, the way his lips tightened, as though he couldn't wait to kiss her there again.

'Nikos,' she murmured, without even knowing what else she wanted to say.

But she didn't need to say anything. He took one look at her then crashed his mouth to hers, all dark and desperate, his hands roaming her body, her legs, her sides, her breasts, coming to catch her face and holding her right where she was, so his mouth could ravage hers until she was a whimpering, desperate mess. 'Please,' she whispered into his mouth, heat forming between her legs, breasts tingling with a desperate need for him to take her.

'Soon,' he promised, pulling his head away so he could see her properly. 'I've never known anyone like you,' he said, but with such darkness that she knew, in a way, he wished he hadn't met her. Because she threatened the life of solitude he'd built. She made him want what he wished to refuse himself.

She lifted a hand, curling her fingers over his cheek. 'It doesn't mean anything,' she said, promising them both that, because they each had their reasons for needing to keep that in mind. 'It's just sex. It doesn't change how you loved your wife, or how much you miss her.'

A muscle jerked in his jaw, and then he was pulling away, sitting in his own seat, fastening his seat belt before running through the pre-flight checks and getting the rotors spinning.

Genevieve's sigh was swallowed by the sound of them lifting off.

To her surprise, he landed the helicopter not on a helipad or at an airport, as she might have predicted, but rather, squarely on the top of an enormous yacht, in the midst of what looked to be—going by the size of the boats—an incredibly prestigious marina. The rotor began to slow down, and Nikos flicked buttons and levers before removing his headset and turning to her, his expression now unreadable. 'Ready, *koukla*?'

Her heart gave a little stammer as she contemplated that. It wasn't too late to change her mind. Could she take another day, and try to work out how to explain this to James? But just remembering the way Nikos had held her—for support—in the lobby set her cheeks aflame. The chemistry between them had instantly flared to life and she had no doubt it would have been captured on camera by some nosy passer-by.

And for all she was determined never to rely on anyone again, there was a part of her that felt relief. Relief at the thought of being able to share her burdens for a while. She'd been alone so long, even within her marriage: aware, constantly, that everything was crumbling down around her and she had no way of fixing it. She'd missed her mother, her father, her old friends, her prospective career, and the man she'd thought her husband to be. Now here was Nikos, with his big broad shoulders, offering to help her. Offering to make her load lighter to carry, to help her manage her ex-husband's response and mitigate his impact in her life.

She would pay him back whatever money was spent, once she was standing on her own two feet. That was a point of pride, and she was determined to do it. But for the rest? Maybe this fake engagement wouldn't just help her. Maybe she could find a way through Nikos's grief, too, and that awful cloak of guilt he carried with him. She was stepping into the second phase of her life; could she encourage him to do the same?

'Yes,' she said, voice unwaveringly clear. 'I'm ready. Let's do this.'

His eyes showed a hint of approval that warmed her chest from the inside out, and a moment later he was stepping out of the helicopter, ducking to avoid the still slowly spinning rotors. Before he could reach her door, though, three men in dark suits, wearing headsets, approached the helicopter. Two moved to Nikos and one to Genevieve, opening the door and saying in accented English, 'Duck your head down.' She did, glad she'd opted to secure her hair in a low bun as a cool breeze whipped past the marina at that moment.

The suited man gestured towards a set of wide stairs. Genevieve cast a glance over her shoulder, her eyes meeting Nikos's even when he was deep in conversation with the other men. He cut off what he was saying immediately and strode towards her, all confident and strong, still her Greek island mountain man, beneath the contours of that incredibly fine suit.

The helipad was on the aft upper deck, and beyond it was a spa and some sun loungers. Beyond these, there was a set of sliding glass doors, which the man in the suit activated by swiping a card across them.

'Tight security,' Genevieve murmured, with a glance up at Nikos.

He simply nodded once, at the same time he put his hand in the small of her back and a whole kaleidoscope of butterflies fluttered to life inside her stomach.

Once inside, Genevieve almost lost her footing. The luxury of the yacht was beyond compare. From shiny teak surfaces to white leather furniture, enormous windows showing the twinkling lights of the other boats and, beyond them, the city. They walked through the room with Nikos barely reacting, so she knew that, for him, this was normal, and ordinary. The contrast to his cabin on the island was the strongest she could imagine. There, he'd been stripped back to his most basic elements, surviving through his grit, and ability to pluck fish from the ocean. Here, he had every luxury one could want, including, by the looks of it, an army of staff.

Having cut through the room, they reached the top of a sweeping staircase, carpeted in beige, with gold handrails. His hand stayed on her back as they descended, arriving in yet another palatial living area, this one with a grand piano, and more creamy white leather sofas.

'It's beautiful,' she said, frowning a little, because she had never been up close with this kind of wealth. 'Truly, Nikos.'

She glanced up at him to see a muscle jerking in his jaw, as though he was clenching his teeth.

'I mean, it's no stone cabin in the woods,' she joked. 'But it's pretty nice.'

At that, he flicked her a grin, and her heart twisted in her chest cavity. A man in a suit entered and approached a low-set coffee table in the middle of the room. She realised, belatedly, that a bottle of champagne sat in an ice bucket, with two glasses beside it. There was also a small tray of chocolate-dipped strawberries, which reminded Genevieve that she hadn't eaten much in the last two days. Her stomach gave a dip of hunger.

The man in the suit unfoiled the top of the bottle and then turned to Nikos. 'May I, sir?'

Nikos nodded once, staying where he was, at Genevieve's side, as the staff member uncorked the champagne then poured two perfect glasses, before discreetly leaving again.

'You have a small army working on here,' Genevieve remarked as Nikos moved towards the champagne flutes and picked them up.

'It takes a small army to keep it running.'

The yacht was the size of a hotel, and undoubtedly a significant investment. It made sense that he would maintain it properly, to make sure it didn't lose value through neglect.

'Is it always ready for you, like this?'

'Not with champagne,' he said, handing her a glass. Their fingers brushed and a thousand sparks ignited in her bloodstream, reminding her of the way she'd tried so hard, that first night in his cabin, to avoid touching him. Even then, she'd known there was something cataclysmic about his touch.

'To our engagement,' he said, holding his drink towards hers.

Genevieve's heart lurched fully then, almost leaping out of her body. She blamed a combination of factors. The champagne, his suit, the luxurious yacht, the warm, moody lighting, but, for the briefest hint of a moment, when he said the word 'engagement' a part of her forgot that it was fake. And forgot that she never wanted to get married again, that she never wanted to put her heart and life in the hands of another person.

'Fake engagement,' she heard herself correct, with a tight smile that earned an answering flicker of his lips. Her heart twisted back into place.

'Of course. There is nothing fake about this, however,' he said, reaching into the breast pocket of his suit and removing a black velvet box.

Memories of James's proposal slammed into her, and

she hated that he had that power. That he would always have that moment in her life, her brain. The way he'd taken her to a celebrity-studded restaurant to make sure the moment would be captured on camera—a wonderful political opportunity for a man who cared so much about his image. Bitterness washed over her, but it did not last long.

Not when she saw the ring. It was clearly an enormous diamond, but it was the lightest blue in colour, shaped like a raindrop. Her eyes lifted to his. Had he chosen it because of the rain that had fallen on that night? The rain and storm that had brought her to him?

Or, more likely, it had simply been what he could find at short notice. The gem itself was surrounded by a circlet of white diamonds, and when he removed it from the box and slid it onto her trembling finger, she fully appreciated the size of the thing, for it almost came up to her knuckle.

'It's…incredible,' she said, staring down at it with a strange feeling that she might cry.

'Your eyes are this exact colour,' he said, putting paid to any idea she might have held that his choice had been random. Her spine tingled with an electrical current as he put the box down on the table and then clinked his glass to hers once more.

But Genevieve felt completely twisted, caught between the illusion of this and reality. Between what she knew had to be her path in life, and what she was glimpsing might just be her fantasy and deepest desire.

For this to be real.

She clenched her champagne glass tighter, a stern voice roaring to life in her mind, warning her off such foolish delusions. She'd already had her heart badly broken by seeing things that weren't there. Nikos had always been honest with her—if not about his wife, about his unavailability. No matter what she might feel and want, he was not interested in anything longer term. She couldn't get swept up in wanting more. No matter how tempting it was.

'I've never thought of that,' she said, sipping her champagne, simply to do something other than speak—lest the words she was thinking tumble out of her mouth.

'It was almost the first thing I noticed about you.'

But he was making it so hard to remember that this was fake. *It's just sex.* She had to cling to that lifeline, to keep it emblazoned in her mind. *It doesn't mean anything.*

'I thought you should have the ring on tonight, as we will undoubtedly be photographed.'

It should have made her feel better, to know that his gift of the ring was linked to their ruse, after all. He saw a weird sort of salvation in getting Genevieve out from under James's shadow, and so he was going to play his part to perfection.

Because Nikos was driven by a torturous guilt, and in fixing this for Genevieve, he thought he could alleviate some of it. Or at least not feel more of it.

'Do you find that strange?'

'The publicity?'

She nodded once.

'I live on my own, in a cabin on an island. What do you think?'

She smiled at that. What she wouldn't give to go back to that cabin… 'Has it always been like this?'

For a moment, his expression darkened, and his jaw grew tight, so she knew she'd hit a sore point. She reached out, putting a hand on his arm. 'You don't have to answer.'

His eyes lanced hers, his features grim. 'It started with my marriage. I had been very successful, professionally, already, and Isabella…she enjoyed the attention that came from being my wife.' He looked past Genevieve's shoulder. 'She courted the media, arranged interviews with high-end, glossy magazines, attended glamorous events and parties. It had the unintended consequence of turning us into tabloid fodder. As my business successes continued, and my wealth became unusual, the press interest likewise increased.' He shifted his gaze back to her face, his eyes stormy once more. 'And when she died, it was as though a pack of vultures had found a fresh carcass. They were everywhere I went. So I went away.'

Genevieve shook her head softly. 'You don't have to answer this, either,' she said, moving closer because it didn't feel right to have this conversation and not be touching him. 'But how did she…?'

'A car accident.'

Genevieve reached up and cupped his stubbled cheek. 'Why do you blame yourself for that, Nikos? An accident is an accident.'

He closed his eyes briefly and she felt his pain as though it were her own. She moved her hand from his cheek to his back, curving it behind his spine and stroking him slowly.

'She had been upset, on the phone, only an hour before she died. She wanted me to come home, but I was working. I was in the midst of negotiating to buy a string of golf resorts across Europe—I had been negotiating the deal for months, and it had come to the final stages. She was furious.'

Genevieve made a clucking sound of sympathy.

'I grew up so poor, Genevieve. After my father's death...' His throat shifted and he shook his head. 'On the island, you asked about the choices my mother had to make. I didn't realise, at first, what she resorted to, in order for us to survive.'

Genevieve blinked up at him, waiting, feeling the way he was opening up to her, sharing himself.

'Selling herself,' he muttered. 'It was her only option.'

Genevieve closed her eyes on a wave of pity.

'I was too young to help, and she died before I turned my life around.'

Genevieve reached out, putting a hand on his forearm. His jaw only tightened.

'Then all of a sudden, I was making money, hand over fist. More money than you can possibly imagine. I didn't care about things like this.' He gestured to the yacht. 'It was about each deal, each metric of success, that made me feel I'd come so far from the boy I'd been. That made me feel safe, like I would never again know that kind of poverty. I can't explain it properly, but growing up like that, it shaped the man I am today. No matter what amount of wealth I have, I have spent years feeling as though that poverty is right there, a shadow waiting to swallow me back into it.'

'I understand,' Genevieve murmured. 'Once my dad died, we struggled, too. It was such a stark contrast to how it had been before. So when I met James and he love-bombed me with expensive gifts and amazing experiences, I got totally caught up in that lifestyle.'

Their eyes held for a long moment of shared understanding. 'But you walked away.'

'That's what I've been trying to tell you. I walked

away, because I couldn't possibly stay. I believe, in my heart of hearts, that Isabella would have divorced you, if she'd been as miserable as you believe.'

'The arguments—'

She sighed. 'Arguments are just a way of communicating.'

He shook his head. 'I never listened.'

'You listened. You just didn't agree.'

'She told me what she needed.'

Genevieve compressed her lips, ignoring, for now, the glaring rejoinder: but what about *your* needs?

'I still don't know why you blame yourself,' she said, quietly. Wishing she could fix this for him, with the click of her fingers.

'She was driving to my office,' Nikos said, after such a long silence Genevieve wasn't sure if he'd return to the subject. 'She missed a stop sign. A car was coming through the intersection and to avoid hitting them, she swerved. Her car wrapped around a pole. Isabella died instantly.'

'Oh, Nikos,' she said, tears forming in her eyes.

'There was no investigation. She'd run a stop sign and died.'

Genevieve nodded, knowing he wasn't finished yet.

'When I got home, much later that night, I saw the whisky bottle, on the kitchen counter, with a single glass beside it. Her lipstick on the rim.' His eyes were boring into Genevieve's and, in their depths, she saw the plea he wouldn't voice. *Forgive me.* 'I drove her to drink, and then she was coming to the office, undoubtedly to finish the argument I'd refused to have. She used to hate that I wouldn't fight back. That I wouldn't lose my temper.' His face contorted into a mask of sheer pain. 'You can have no idea how much that has tormented me. How often I have reflected on my choices, the way I treated her.'

Genevieve's tears fell unashamedly now. She shook her head a little, unsure what to say. 'Nothing good can come from hating yourself. You can't change the past.'

'I'm aware of that. And I'm not looking for anything good. In fact, that is the exact opposite of what I want.'

'You want to be miserable and alone.'

'As she was.'

Genevieve sighed heavily. 'It sounds to me as though she loved you a great deal, Nikos. She stayed with you, when she could have left. You need to stop torturing yourself.'

But she could see by his reaction that he had no intention of doing any such thing. 'Let's go to dinner, *agape*. It's time to let the world see you've moved on from your ex-husband.'

She didn't dare ask if he would ever move on from his late wife. Besides, she had the answer, and it sat in her gut like an oversized lead balloon.

CHAPTER ELEVEN

EVERYTHING ABOUT THE night had been scripted to perfection. From the limousine that had whisked them through the streets of Athens to one of the most prestigious restaurants in the city, with striking views of the Parthenon, and the golden glowing city beyond. Whether by request or happenstance, they had been placed on an intimatc table on a private balcony, with overhead heating to keep them toasty warm. It hadn't been necessary. Just the way Nikos's legs had brushed hers had lit a fire in Genevieve's soul that only he could extinguish—later, in his own, sweet time.

Though their table had been private, their entry to the restaurant had taken them past a dozen paparazzi, and once inside, she'd been aware of several patrons surreptitiously lifting their phones to snatch photos of the reclusive Greek billionaire and the woman on his arm. Genevieve realised later that the way she'd held his forearm would have displayed her engagement ring—without her intending to—to perfection, leaving no one in any doubt as to what their relationship was. There was also the possessive way Nikos had kept an arm around her waist as they'd left the restaurant, and Genevieve had leaned into his warm side, not caring about the photographers so much as being near him.

The same car had returned them to the marina, to her surprise, where they'd boarded the yacht using the side-facing gangplank. Once they were onboard, it had been retracted, giving them total privacy and security.

'Is this where you stay, when you come to Athens?' she asked as he brewed a pot of dark coffee and came to sit on the sofa beside her. He poured two small cups of the sticky, dark liquid, then sat back in the seat, casually draping his arm along the back so his fingers brushed her shoulder and she tingled.

She hesitated for only the briefest moment before curling her legs up beside her and leaning close to him, her eyes fanning shut as she listened to the solid beating of his heart.

'No. In fact, I've never stayed here before.'

She opened her eyes and glanced up at him. 'Oh. Why not?'

He held her gaze a long moment, then reached for his coffee, taking a sip. He placed the cup on his knee, before returning his eyes to her face. 'I bought the yacht a month before the accident.' His voice had a hoarse quality to it. 'It was intended as a gift, for Isabella.' He closed his eyes then. 'A guilt gift. I knew she wasn't happy, that she liked nice things. I thought—'

Genevieve nodded. She understood. His guilt and grief, the knowledge that he had made the wrong choices then.

'I was trying to keep the peace.'

'And she didn't like it?'

'I didn't get a chance to give it to her. I kept waiting for the right moment—a day in which we didn't argue, a moment when things felt as they once had. Happy and normal, easy. It never came.'

Genevieve placed her hand on his taut, muscular abdomen, inwardly marvelling at the sheer strength of this man.

'So where do you stay?' she asked, rather than pushing him to continue talking about his wife.

She felt him tighten, his belly drawing inwards as though he'd taken a deep breath. 'Our home.'

Her heart wrenched at the pain loaded into those two simple words.

'You lived in Athens?'

He nodded once.

'What's it like?'

'Exactly as it was, before she died,' he admitted. 'I don't go there often. I can't bear to. But there are certain dates in the year when it feels right to remember.'

'To remember your wife, or remember what you perceive you did to her?'

His eyes showed surprise at her perceptiveness. 'Both,' he admitted, after a beat. 'Mainly the latter. It is hard to allow myself to remember her without also recalling the pain I inflicted, by being so careless.'

Genevieve shook her head. 'You know, I wonder if your memory is a little flawed.'

'It's not, believe me.'

'I believe you're remembering things as you think they were, but our memories are fallible, shaped by our present perceptions. I've known you less than a week, yet I know you're not the kind of person who'd willingly, knowingly hurt another.'

A muscle ticced in his jaw. 'She told me how she felt. I refused to listen.'

'Did she listen to how you felt?' Genevieve said, gently, aware that the last thing she wanted to do was criticise his poor, late wife. 'Did your wants change from when you were dating, to married? Or were you always a workaholic?'

He glanced away, towards the windows.

'Because it sounds to me like she knew what she was getting, and just wanted you to be different, once you were married. People don't change.'

'No,' he agreed, gruffly. 'They don't.' His hand moved to her hair, gently running over it. She shivered at the small, intimate gesture. 'I wish I had, though.'

'She loved you, Nikos. She stayed with you; she fought to be with you. There was enough in your marriage to make her want to stay. Take it from someone who spent almost every day of her marriage planning to leave. Hold onto that, not the arguments, not the blame. Focus on the good memories—I'm convinced that's what she would have wanted.'

He stood then, abruptly, unsettling her as he strode across the room and placed his coffee cup down on a side table, and stared out of the glass windows that showed a view of the distant city. His back moved with each intake of breath. Then, slowly, he turned to face her, his whole body radiating tension.

'I want to help you, Genevieve. I hate what your ex is doing to you. But for the duration of this fake engagement, let us agree that you will not try to make me feel better about my own failings. I do not need it; I do not want it.'

She ran the gamut of emotions. At first, it was easy to

feel hurt. She'd been coldly rejected by James so many times that her first instinct was to see the same treatment in Nikos. Except there was nothing cold in Nikos, nor his words. For all he was holding onto his emotions with ruthless self-control, she could sense his feelings thrumming around the cabin. The desperation with which he clung to his guilt, almost as a protective mechanism to save him from fully feeling grief. He was using his wife's death as an excuse, to stop him from moving on with his life, and to protect himself from ever loving—and losing—another person. She could see it so clearly, all of a sudden, and the fact he had his head in the sand about it infuriated her. So much so she stood, and weaved through the furniture, cutting across to him in a scant few seconds, and trying to rally her thoughts.

Trying to calm down, as well, to remember that, in her marriage, she had become expert at holding her temper and her tongue.

Those skills seemed to have deserted her now.

'I don't appreciate being told how I can act,' she said, the words calm enough, though they vibrated slightly. 'James spent our entire marriage sculpting my behaviour and personality, to be the perfect political wife. I will not endure the same from you.'

'You are not my wife,' he pointed out, and now she fully understood what he was doing. Picking a fight with her to push her away. Denying that there was anything real in this relationship because he couldn't bear to face the alternative: that something was happening between them neither wanted nor had expected. Genevieve was terrified of that, too, but at least she was willing to face it head-on.

'No,' she agreed. 'But I'm a grown woman, intelligent and perceptive and I can say whatever I want,' she said. 'You are being so selfish, to wallow in guilt and consign your wife's memory to that alone. Why not talk about how wonderful she was? How clever and loyal, talk about her goals and aspirations? Why dwell only on your guilt? On what you think you did wrong, and the arguments that led you to have?'

'Don't,' he ground out, eyes boring into hers.

But she lifted a hand to his chest, her fingers splayed wide. 'You can't process her loss. You're just treading water, keeping your head in the sand, because you're afraid to move on.'

His nostrils flared. 'What gives you any right to think you know so much about me? We've just met.'

'Am I wrong?' she demanded, lifting up onto her tiptoes and grabbing his face with both hands, holding him still, their eyes locked.

His lips parted on a rush of breath.

'Am I wrong?' she repeated fiercely.

'It doesn't matter,' he said, dropping his head, so their mouths were almost touching. 'Whether you are right or wrong, it is my life, and how I choose to live it is my business. I would ask you again to keep your opinions on this matter to yourself.'

And before she could answer, he was kissing her with all the pent-up passion, frustration, grief, guilt and need that was flooding his system, kissing her as though it could somehow fix everything. And she was kissing him back in the same way, her mouth mashing to his, their tongues meshing, teeth clashing as they let passion control them completely. His hands, so big, broad and strong, curved around her bottom and pushed her against his erection, so she groaned into his mouth.

'Please,' she moaned, moving her hips as those same hands moved to her dress and ruched it in his palms before lifting it, pushing it over her head, leaving her naked except for a lace thong. He cursed against her skin as he moved his mouth to the curve of her neck and kissed her there, as his hands fumbled between them, unfastening his trousers and freeing his cock from the confines of fabric. A moment later, he was lifting her, wrapping her legs around his waist, and moving one step forward, so her back was bracing against the cold glass window as he drove into her in a single motion that had them both crying out on a wave of sheer, giddy relief.

'Nikos,' she cried, digging her fingernails into his shoulders, gripping him hard and tight, the pleasure of his possession unlike anything she'd ever known, even from this man. It was the heightened tension they'd felt in the lead-up, the argument that had been both hyper-emotional but also a form of foreplay. Or maybe that had been the time they'd spent apart, after having each other completely to themselves, on the island. But when he drove into her, it was like the bursting of a bank, and she was incapable of doing anything to stem the tide. She surrendered to it completely; let it catch her and take her out to sea.

'It is bad enough,' he said, dropping his mouth to her breast and flicking her nipple with his tongue, while his hand moved between her legs and brushed her clit, 'that you make me feel like this when we have sex. That in this moment, I feel as though I am a god on earth, that all is right. It is so much more than I deserve, more than I told myself I would ever have.' He moved his mouth to her other nipple and drew it into his mouth sharply, sucking hard enough that she cried out at the agonising form of pleasure. It was almost too much to bear.

'You do deserve—'

'I deserve nothing,' he said, dragging his mouth back to hers and kissing her with the same fevered passion as the tide of pleasure burst around her again, so she cried out at the orgasm he delivered her so swiftly and easily. 'Only the knowledge that this is temporary allows me to give into this. Just for now, not for ever. When you are gone, everything will once more be as it's meant to be.'

He would have had no way of seeing the tears that sprang to her eyes, because she squeezed them shut and sought his mouth with hers, trying to kiss into him the peace she wished he could feel. How could she make him understand?

James was not rocking in a corner in their apartment in Washington, thinking of all the ways in which he'd failed her. He was not bemoaning the poor choices he'd made during their marriage. Because he was the worst kind of man. But Nikos? Nikos was all good. The evidence of that was in his guilt, his grief, and his inability to forgive himself. She wished she could make him understand.

But if there was one thing she'd learned through and through, in her marriage, it was that one person could not change another. Not unless they truly wished to be different. And she had no reason to suspect, let alone hope, that Nikos ever would. He'd chosen his path and, unless he chose to stray from it, she had to leave him to walk it. Alone, as he so clearly wanted.

It wasn't until much later, in the early hours of the

morning, when naked with limbs entwined, wrapped in the luxurious million-thread-count sheets of the master bedroom, with the yacht gently bobbing from side to side, and Nikos asleep beside her, that Genevieve realised she hadn't so much as thought of what *she* wanted. And a fear began to curl through her, wrapping around her organs, making it hard to breathe, as she faced the reality of their situation: she hadn't protected herself. Not enough. She'd told herself she would never fall in love with another man, that she would never want what had the potential to hurt her, and yet, in a few short days, she'd fallen utterly and completely under the spell of someone who was determined to be miserable for the rest of his life.

Talk about a glutton for punishment.

It was barely five in the morning when he became aware of the buzzing of his phone, on the bedside table. He reached for it quickly, not wanting to wake Genevieve, who was fast asleep in the crook of his arm. They'd spent hours making love the night before—hard and fast at first, filled with pent-up emotions and frustrations, and then long and slow, with him delighting in delivering the best kind of torture, driving her wild and then bringing her back from the precipice, showing her what her body was capable of, how prolonging release could enhance pleasure exponentially. And then, as proof of how far she'd come since they'd first met, he'd watched as she'd pleasured herself, her cheeks flushed as she'd tipped over the edge, crying his name and reaching for him, even then, wanting—needing—more. Despite that, the buzzing of the phone had woken him, and made him aware that he was already hard and aching for her anew.

He would have silenced the call and turned off his phone, except for the fact that, at the last moment, he saw the call was coming in from Washington, and he had a premonition that made the hairs on the back of his neck stand on end.

He eased himself from the bed, walked as swiftly from the room as he could and then swiped the phone to answer.

'Konstantinou.'

Silence met his pronouncement.

'Yes?' he barked down the line, aware who it was likely to be.

'Senator James Wilson,' came the voice he already hated from the man he loathed and despised. 'We need to talk.'

'Do we?' Nikos drawled, moving deeper into the yacht, further from the bedroom suite. 'About what?'

'You, and my wife.'

'Ex-wife. And I think you mean my fiancée.'

Silence. But a silence that was loaded with animosity; Nikos felt it and understood it. But what grace could he give this man? He'd had Genevieve in his life, his bed, her loyalty and love in his hands to treasure, and he'd treated her like a piece of dirt. For all Nikos had made mistakes in his marriage, it had never been intentional, nor cruel. The effects had been the same—he'd hurt his wife—but that had never been his aim. Far from it.

'Is she there?'

The question was flooded with angry indignation. There was no way Nikos was going to pass the phone to Genevieve. 'She's sleeping.'

A hiss—clear fury. 'You don't know what you're getting into.'

'Do I seem like someone who makes poor decisions?'

'Have Genevieve call me.'

'For what purpose? You're divorced. Whatever you once shared is over.'

'What's the matter, Konstantinou? You jealous?'

He laughed then. A low, soft rumble. 'Of a man who does not even know how to please a woman? Oh, yes. My anxiety is off the charts.'

James cursed. 'Get her to call me.'

'I'll do no such thing. Not when it's clear you can't be trusted to play nice.'

'Oh, Genevieve knows I don't play nice—and she knows what's going to happen now. It's her own fault. And yours too, I suppose.'

'What's going to happen now is that you're going to take yourself off and have a long, clear think about whether or not you want me as an enemy,' Nikos said, letting the words fall. 'You know who I am.'

Silence, but there was no need for an answer, anyway. Not when the other man would have to have been living under a rock not to know who Nikos was. 'You can imagine who my contacts are. With a handful of phone calls, I can make sure your political donations dry up—permanently. And I will delight in doing so, believe me.'

'You—can't—'

'Can't I? Would you like to test me?'

A spluttering sound. 'Fuck you,' he shouted.

'You've said that already, Senator. Surely a man of your intelligence can think of something more creative.'

'She's not worth this,' he threw down the phone line. 'She's a cold, frigid—'

'Setting aside the fact I have much evidence to the contrary, if you ever say anything like that about my fiancée again, if you so much as utter her name in anything but the most complimentary of ways, my threat will come to fruition. This is not an idle promise, Senator. I will ruin you in every way you hold dear if you ever make a single move to hurt her. If you threaten or bully her, if you breathe a single word of anything she told you in confidence, when she was trying to make your pathetic marriage work, I will destroy you. If you ever attempt to contact her, if you see her walking on the street and don't immediately turn and go the other way, you will wish, with every fibre of your being, to be someone else entirely. Do I make myself clear?'

The silence that greeted him made the hairs on the back of his neck stand to attention once more.

'I said, do I make myself clear?'

'Yes.' It was belligerent but also, Nikos was certain, terrified.

'Good boy,' he drawled condescendingly. 'Now get back to your hollow little life, screwing shallow, meaningless women, and think about the fact you had someone very special in your life, for a time, and you ruined it. And then, burn in hell.'

He disconnected the call and threw his phone against the cushions of the sofa, his chest puffing up with outrage at even the sound of the man's voice. And then, in the reflection of the windows, he saw a movement that had him turning around, heart ramming hard against his ribs.

CHAPTER TWELVE

SHE UNDERSTOOD THAT he was talking about himself. That the anger he felt towards himself for having not been able to appreciate Isabella was at the root of his defence, but, at the same time, just hearing him say those things to her ex-husband—for clearly that was who was on the other end of the line—set a fire in her soul. Hearing the way he threatened James, promising to ruin him financially and politically, knowing that was probably the most likely to get through to him, had underscored something very simple to Genevieve. For all she had wanted to stand on her own two feet and walk away from James, he was just the kind of misogynistic horror of a man who would only be affected by this sort of thing.

But it wasn't even about James, and it wasn't about Isabella.

The magic of Nikos's words, his passion, his respect, flooded her veins so she was running across the room and hurling herself at him, fighting floods of tears as she practically scrambled up his body and into his arms, so she could kiss him and hold him and thank him as she wrapped her arms around his neck.

Surprise held him still a moment, but then their predictable, reliable passion flared to life and he was kissing her back, holding her now against him, feet off the ground as he moved them to the sofa and laid her down, before bringing his body weight over hers and nudging her thighs apart with his knee.

'I meant every word, Genevieve,' he said, pushing up to stare into her eyes. 'Even when this is over, and you are back in the States, if he so much as calls you, I expect to know about it. If he ever gives you even a hint of trouble—'

'He won't,' she said, and her smile was enormous because, for the first time in a long time, she truly felt that everything would be okay. Her divorce hadn't given her that freedom. James had made sure of it. He'd found a way to extend his control and manipulation, his cold hurtfulness, well after their legal union had been dissolved. She'd left America, and come to Greece, but his shadow had been over her the whole time.

Until now.

'I can never thank you enough.'

He shook his head, his throat shifting, and she held her breath, waiting for him to say whatever he was obviously thinking, but instead, he offered a smile that didn't reach his eyes. 'Thank me by shouting my name as loud as you can, *koukla*. Shout it so loud he can hear it, all the way in Washington.' And he dragged his mouth down her body, to her sex, and proceeded to make it impossible for her to do anything but what he'd suggested.

Over and over his name tripped from her tongue, a poem she was writing and feeling in her heart, both a joy and a burden. He drove her wild with his mouth, and then his hands, and then his mouth, before finally arranging her on the sofa so he could claim her from behind, his whole body intimately connected with hers as his hands came and clutched her breasts, before one roamed to her sex and made her halfway forget her own damned name. Even as he gave her such pleasure, over and over, she heard the words he'd spoken, and felt them like a blade in her side: *Even when this is over.*

And it just served to clarify for Genevieve the truth of her feelings. The problem wasn't that she'd trusted someone with her heart, it was that she'd trusted the wrong someone. She'd given herself to a man who'd never deserved her. But Nikos was so different. He was her perfect other half, in every way, but it was almost impossible to imagine him recognising that, far less accepting it.

Though she knew she loved him, Genevieve was too proud to stay, if she was truly not wanted. Or perhaps it was that she was seeking breadcrumbs of affection, in the form of his trying to prolong this. Either way, when he said, later that afternoon, that they had reservations at another Athens hotspot, she found herself hesitating before saying, 'Nikos, you've done so much for me. But he knows now, and I'm pretty sure he won't be bothering me again. If you wanted…if you want to go back to the island, I won't keep you here.'

His expression had barely shifted, except for a slight darkening in those stunning grey eyes of his. 'He understands his situation, it's true,' he murmured. 'But wouldn't you like to have the fun of making him suffer now?' he asked, lifting a single brow. 'Every photo of us—of you, living your best life, with me—will be like the twisting of a knife. Don't you think you deserve that?'

Genevieve's agreement had nothing to do with James,

though. Whatever Nikos might think, for Genevieve, it was simply a chance to spend more time with Nikos. To lose herself to him, in the hope—albeit a very, very small one—that the more they were together, the more he would see that he deserved this second chance. That the grief he was stubbornly clinging to, the guilt he insisted he must wallow in, were an insult to his late wife, a cruelty to himself, and a deprivation to Genevieve.

'Yes,' she said, simply, and his smile was her reward.

'Then get dressed,' he said, pulling her against his body. 'And let me have the pleasure of watching you.'

Her heart rushed against her ribcage. 'It will be the same dress I wore last night,' she said, with a lift of one shoulder.

'Believe me, I barely notice the clothes you have on—most of my energy is spent imagining how quickly I can remove them.'

Heat flushed her cheeks as he led her to the shared master bedroom, and, rather than watching her get ready, he chose to help her undress, kiss her all over, before slowly, tantalisingly sliding the red slip in place. But as he did so, he removed her lace thong, his eyes clashing with hers.

'For me,' he said, and the heart that was already rushing began to gallop so hard it hurt.

After dinner, when they were back in the limousine, but not yet moving, he pulled her into his lap so her legs straddled him and undid his trousers, eyes hooked to hers as he freed his arousal and said, 'Fuck me, Genevieve.'

'Oh, God,' she groaned, doing exactly that, easing herself over his length and crying out as he filled her so completely and his hands massaged her bottom. His mouth sought her breasts, which were at his mouth's height, but, impatient to taste her, he pulled at the dress she wore, tearing it easily with his enormous hands, so she made a half-laughing sound of surprise.

'I suppose I'll have to go to dinner naked from now on.'

He grinned as he took one of her nipples in his mouth. 'Sounds fine by me.'

But the next morning, after breakfast, she became aware of the yacht's staff moving to and from the gangplank, and when she went to look, with natural curiosity, she saw they were carrying bags and bags, emblazoned with famous fashion labels, as well as hat boxes and shoe boxes. She whirled around to face him, shaking her head. 'Nikos…'

'I felt bad about the dress,' he said, pulling her sharply against his body, so she could tell instantly that he didn't feel a single bit bad about anything that had happened in the car the night before.

'How bad?' she murmured, eyes raking his.

'Awful.' His grin told a totally different story.

'Care to make it up to me?'

Hours later, naked in his bed, Genevieve pushed up onto her elbow, a feeling growing inside her that she wanted to share, but was almost too nervous to voice. And yet, they'd been so intimate, and he'd taught her so much. Surely there was nothing she couldn't ask of him.

'What is it?' he asked, reaching out and indolently flicking one of her nipples, so she bit her lower lip between her teeth. His eyes fell to the gesture, his eyes darkening as he moved swiftly to claim her mouth with his own, and to drag her lower lip between his teeth.

But she was shy suddenly, too shy to say the words. Instead, she pulled away and moved her body over his, kissing his chest and then moving lower, to his hips, her eyes flicking to his frequently, to see how he was reacting. Anxiety spread through her, until she couldn't bear it. He'd kissed her most intimate places so often—several times a day, when they'd been together—he'd driven her wild with his mouth, and she'd yet to do the same to him.

And she knew why.

James's voice had been in her mind. His criticism of her, his derision when she'd tried, had made her too shy to try again. *You're like a cold fish. This is boring.*

But with Nikos, she wanted, desperately, to take him in her mouth. To feel him there and to see him lose control the way she so often did because of his ministrations.

She reached his hip bone and pressed kisses along the ridge there, her eyes flicking to his again, to see dark colour spreading across his cheeks, his expression so still, and watchful.

'Koukla,' he said, with a small shift of his head. She bit into her lip, and his hand moved, cupping her cheek then swiping across her lip, before his thumb pushed between her lips, his eyes following the gesture. 'You don't have to do this.'

'I know.' She moved her mouth away, towards the tip of his cock. 'I want to. It's just… I don't think… I don't know what to do.'

She saw the comprehension in his eyes, the anger that swiftly followed, but he blanked it again, almost immediately. Neither of them wanted James to darken this moment. To be any kind of factor in what they shared.

'Do whatever you want. I'm yours, Genevieve. For right now, here, I'm all completely yours.'

And she took him in her mouth with a heart that was both full and broken. Full because what they shared defied so many hopes she'd held, but also broken, by his subtle, frequent reminders that this was temporary, when she wanted, more than anything, for it to be for keeps.

Everything he'd ever thought he knew about the world split and exploded as she moved her mouth down his length, struggling at first with the size of him and then growing in confidence—and pleasure—at the way it felt to take him like this. She moved her hips with wanton need as she lifted and dropped her head until his whole body was flooded with electricity and heat was flooding his balls, threatening to burst from him.

'Stop,' he said, barely able to speak, the word rasped from his body.

The hurt in her eyes made him want to reach right across the ocean and slam his fist into her vile ex's face. That he could have undermined her sexual confidence so completely was abhorrent. Far from being frigid, Genevieve was sensual and warm, and the more they were together, the more her confidence grew, so he saw now a woman who, not only sought her pleasure, but delighted in it—in taking and giving. In the back of his mind, he knew that was because of him, and that he would always be glad to have given that to her.

'Is it—wrong?'

'*Christo*, no, but I am about to come, and I do not want to do so in your mouth.'

She frowned. 'You don't?'

He grabbed her under the arms and pulled her up his body, shaking his head when their eyes were level. 'For your sake, believe me. For your sake.'

'But I—'

He shook his head once. He didn't want to overwhelm her, not when she was still learning so much about what she liked.

'Let me feel you like this,' he insisted as he held her hips and thrust into her, already spilling a little of his seed, because of how close he'd been. 'You are heaven on earth, do you know that?'

She dropped her head and kissed him, and said something he didn't quite catch into his mouth, something whispered and low, that he didn't ask her to repeat. Perhaps even then, on some level, he'd known things were getting out of hand. But it felt too incredibly good to stop…

She was used to the thundering of her heart, after they'd made love. Used to the way it felt as though it were going to launch clear out of her chest, because no way could her ribs stand up to that kind of punishment. But this time, as she lay in his arms, breath rushing from her lungs, body sated—for now—she knew that her heart was racing for another reason.

I love you so much.

The words had just dropped out of her, whispered from her straight into his mouth, pressed against him without her intention—and without his reaction. The words had been pulled right from the centre of her being, sucked out of her by the truth of her feelings, and they sat in her throat again now, begging to be spoken. To be spoken again and again, shouted, until he understood that this was not just sex, and it wasn't going anywhere.

'Nikos,' she murmured, glancing up at him, to see his face in profile set in firm lines, a slight frown on his face.

As if he'd heard and was processing? Rejecting? Or was he thinking about something else?

If he had been anything like James, she would have stayed quiet. Fear had been her constant companion, and she'd shrunk herself down so completely, hidden who she was from the man who seemed to live to reject her.

But Nikos was not James, and, if nothing else, he deserved to know that she loved him. If he chose to walk away from her, and go back to his isolated island, his life of self-imposed misery, then he would. But at least he'd be going with the knowledge that she loved him—and one day, he might even accept that he was worthy of that love.

He angled his face so their gazes met, and her heart stammered harder. 'I meant what I said,' she murmured, reaching up to cup his cheek.

'And what exactly did you say?'

She swallowed, to see if the words would dislodge, but they refused, so she surrendered to their agency. 'I love you, so much.'

She felt his response. The tightening of his body, the tensing of his muscles. Even before he shook his head, she knew the rejection was coming. 'Genevieve—' His voice sounded disbelieving. 'Why would you say that?'

She scrambled to sitting, pulling the sheet with her, to cover her breasts. 'Because I want you to know it,' she said honestly. 'I'm not asking you to love me back. I'm not asking you to say that. But I need you to know that somewhere along the way, I fell in love with you, and I have absolutely no regrets about that. Because you are good and kind, strong and noble, generous and thoughtful. I love everything about you, Nikos, except for how hard you are on yourself, but even that is a mark of your goodness.'

'Don't,' he groaned, pushing out of the bed and striding across the room, before spinning around to face her. 'Don't say these things. What did I ask of you, when we began this fake engagement?'

She flinched a little at his reckless use of the word 'fake'. As if to echo her rejection of the concept, she began to twirl her engagement ring.

'Am I not allowed to be honest with you?'

He dropped his head forward, staring at the floor. 'Tell me you love me, if you absolutely must, but don't ever imply that I deserve it.' His eyes lifted to hers. 'Don't you understand? The more you offer, the more guilt I feel. After what I did to her, I could *never* deserve you.'

Tears welled in her eyes. 'She stayed with you,' Genevieve said. 'You didn't force her to do that. You didn't make her remain married. She *wanted* your marriage, and she wanted you. You need to accept that.'

'I will not talk about my marriage, or my wife, with you right now.'

She flinched again. 'Because you know I'll make you see the truth, and you can't handle it. You can't handle the fact that the more time you spend with me, the less you hate yourself. Give me another week and you'll never want to go back to the island,' she challenged, eyes meeting his. 'A week after that and you'll be ready to admit that you love me, too.'

He took a step back, a stagger, his face blanching. 'You don't know what you're talking about.'

'I think I do.'

'We've just met.'

'So?'

'So how can you possibly think we are in love, after less than a week?'

'Do you doubt that I love you?'

'I think you're running from trauma, and you ran into my arms. I think I gave you pleasure for the first time in your life, and freedom from your husband. Those are two very seductive, powerful gifts. But gratitude is not tantamount to love. Great sex is not love.'

'You think I don't know that?' She pushed out of the bed then, staring at him with a heart that was weeping. 'You think I'm saying I love you because you can basically give me an orgasm just by looking at me?'

'Perhaps.'

She swore softly, under her breath. She hadn't expected him to return her declaration, but she'd at least expected him to accept it.

'You're wrong,' she said.

'Or maybe it's because you spent three years trying to love a complete jackass that your heart just desperately wants to be put to use now.'

She shook her head. 'Stop.'

His eyes flashed with wildness, and she recognised the cause of it. The panic he was feeling, because she was getting under his skin. Not just with her love, but with the things she kept saying about his marriage, showing him that his wife had loved him, regardless of his long hours and her frustrations there.

'You don't have to tell me you love me. You don't have to give me *anything* you don't want to. But at least let me speak what I feel. I spent my entire marriage squashing myself into a ball, metaphorically speaking, hiding how I felt and what I wanted, pretending to be something I never was. So let me always be honest with you. I love you. From the bottom of my heart, with every single part of me, I absolutely, unfailingly love and adore you. I would spend the rest of my life worshipping you, if you'd let me.' A tear slid down her cheek. 'But I also spent my marriage trying to make a man love me, who never had any intention of doing so. I will not make that mistake again. Either love me freely, or let me go.'

CHAPTER THIRTEEN

'GO,' HE SAID, closing his eyes so he didn't have to see her reaction. Closing his eyes against the bitter, shredding feeling of regret and grief. Of knowing that, once again, he'd taken something beautiful and destroyed it. He doubted he would ever get over the sense of regret.

Cowardice was not his natural bent, however, so Nikos forced himself to open his eyes and look at her, to see the anguish in her face. He looked at her in the way he'd never been brave or aware enough to do with Isabella. Her complaints had fallen on deaf ears. But with Genevieve, her every word, tortured by the fact he would never return her feelings, though whispered, landed with a thud.

'Okay,' she said, nodding slowly, turning her back on him then moving to the wardrobe. He stood his ground, even when his body was desperately trying to propel him forwards. She returned a moment later, wearing the shorts and shirt she'd had on when she'd washed ashore on his island. His gut rolled. 'I don't know how,' she said, lifting one shoulder, looking every bit as vulnerable as she'd been that night. 'I don't have a phone. I can't call a car. Would you—?'

'I'll arrange it, of course,' he said, rocks in his gut rolling together to form a dusty sediment that flooded his whole body. 'Where would you like to go to?'

'I still have the room in Katanos. Can you send me there?'

Can you send me there?

Every single shred of good he'd done her was undermined by the vulnerability in that question. He moved then, crossing the room and putting his hands on her hips. 'Genevieve,' he said, but she shook her head and stepped away from him.

'Just leave it,' she asked breathily. 'I don't think we need to say anything more. We both know how we feel.'

But she didn't know how he felt. She couldn't. Not when those feelings were all so jumbled and tangled, a horrible knotty nightmare of what he wanted and needed, and needed to forbid himself from taking. The pledge he'd made himself on his wife's death he considered to be unbreakable.

Nothing had changed that; nothing ever could.

'Very well. I'll take you back to Katanos.'

'No,' she said, quickly shaking her head again. 'Not you. I think it's better if we say goodbye here. I can take the train. I just need someone to drive me to the station.'

'I'll—'

'No, not you,' she stressed. 'Please, Nikos. Just let me go, okay?'

What could he say to that? She'd given him two options. Love her, or let her go. He'd chosen the latter with barely a moment's hesitation. And he would have a lifetime to live with the consequences.

* * *

The trip to the other side of Greece took almost six hours, and from there, she had to take a cab to her hotel, which was another twenty minutes. By the time she arrived, she was exhausted, having not slept more than a few snatched hours on the train over, and even those had been tormented by dreams of Nikos, by her desire for him, her aching for him, her grief for him. Because he deserved so much more, but he would probably never see that.

She would have spent a lifetime trying to make him see it, if he'd let her.

If he'd fought to keep her in his life, in any capacity, she would have stayed. But he was too good and decent for that, too traumatised by his belief that his marriage had, for his wife, been purely bad.

She stared out on Katanos as the taxi approached her hotel, but already, she was mentally pulling herself away from Greece, and the life she'd suddenly built here. It wasn't real. It couldn't be, when the feelings were so one-sided. Besides, she had a life in America she needed to return to. The business of finding a job and finally putting her college education to good use, and, most importantly, the getting on with her own life.

In a way, she supposed she should have been grateful. She'd arrived in Greece feeling emotionally bruised and battered by James, but now she barely thought of the man she'd once been married to. All of her heartache, all of her heart, belonged to Nikos Konstantinou, and always would.

It was the sight of her engagement ring on the edge of the basin that finally got through to him. She'd left, he'd watched her go, but it was seeing that ring—which, for him, had been so meaningfully chosen—discarded as a totem of their time together that really hammered it home to him that she was gone, and because of him.

That he'd hurt her.

Failed her.

That in some ways, he was no better than her husband.

Or wouldn't be, if he didn't at least send her away with more than a panic-driven insistence that she leave.

Not five minutes later, the rotors of the helicopter were turning and he was lifting up, over Athens, his mind already focused on Katanos, and the beautiful woman he knew he'd find there.

Genevieve had been sleeping most of the day. Grief, exhaustion and depression had all caught up with her, and her brain had wrapped her in a protective mechanism, all but sedating her into a deep slumber, so she felt as though she were miles beneath the surface of the earth. So at first, she didn't hear the banging on the door. But then, like a mallet or a ratchet, it burst through her dreams, meaning she woke up disorientated and alert, her pulse thrumming with alarm as her body wondered what was wrong.

'Genevieve?'

Even through the door and across the carpeted floor, she knew instantly that it was Nikos. From the sound of his voice, but also from the ache in her heart. She moved quickly, pushing back the sheet and crossing the small hotel room, with absolutely no idea what time it was. The sun was up, but, as far as she knew, it could have been anywhere from midday to sundown.

She wrenched open the door and stared at him, her insides twisting with love and familiarity, with the recognition that she was looking back at her other half.

'Don't go,' he said, drawing her into his arms and holding her hard against him. Hope flared in her chest, soaring like an eagle, out of control and brilliant. 'Don't go like this,' he said, taking that hope and strangling it into nothing.

'What does that mean?' she asked, pushing back to look up into his face. The expression there almost wrenched her apart.

'I can't let you go,' he ground out. 'I thought I could, but I need to know that, no matter where you are, you're okay. I need to know you're safe, protected. I need that like I need air.'

Her stomach dropped to her toes. 'What are you saying?'

'I'm saying I can't be with you,' he said, cupping her cheeks and staring down at her with every bit of intensity he possessed. 'You know me better than I know myself; you know why I feel as I do.'

She swept her eyes closed against the assault of his desperation. 'You love me,' she whispered, knowing it was true.

'I can't be with you,' he said, simply.

'That's not an answer.'

'Isn't it?'

Her eyes blinked open to face his and she saw the resolution there, the determination to stick to this viewpoint, no matter how painful it was to both.

'But the thought of you losing your way again, of you ending up with someone like James, someone worse, it would kill me, Genevieve. No matter where you are, you are a part of me. I have to know you're okay.'

'I'll be okay,' she lied, because in that moment she felt as though she never would be again.

'Let me take care of you,' he said, and something tightened inside her, like screws against her ribs.

'Take care of me how?' To her own ears, the coldness was obvious in her tone, but he clearly didn't hear it—or heed it.

'Let me set you up in your own place, take away any financial worries. Let me care for you. And occasionally, God, Genevieve, God help me for my weakness, let me see you and remember that when I'm with you, I genuinely feel as though I am what you say. Let me see myself as you do, from time to time.'

'From time to time,' she murmured, imagining the world he described with a sense of overwhelming barrenness. The idea of living in that awful state of purgatory, just as he was on the island, one foot between both their worlds.

'I cannot give you what you want, but I can give you so much, if you'll let me.'

She took a step backwards, to put space between them, but he followed, and closed the door behind them, so she startled at the sound of it slamming.

'Please,' he said, and she knew it wasn't a word he used often. It dug right into her heart. She blinked away, turning to look at the view, towards the island, imagining the future she really wanted. Side by side with him, no matter where, no matter how they lived.

'I can't accept that,' she said, swallowing past a lump in her throat. 'It's not enough.'

'It's more than you have now.'

She turned back to him, her lips quivering in an attempt at a weak smile. 'Is it? I have my independence, Nikos, and I fought so hard for it. I would *never* sacrifice that again, except for the deepest kind of mutual love. How have you so fundamentally misunderstood me?'

'Genevieve—'

'No.' She shook her head, holding up a hand. 'There are only two things I want in this world, and I had my whole marriage to recognise that. I deserve to be loved. Wholly, fully, without restraint. Messy, consuming, warts-and-all love.' She tilted her chin, daring him with her defiant expression to contradict her. 'And I deserve to be with someone who knows that I have what it takes to stand on my own two feet.' The last one really hurt. 'With James, I gave up my independence because he said he wanted to look after me, and I ended up with no agency, and no options. If you think I would ever make that mistake again, even with someone I love as much as I do you, then you really don't get what I've been through.'

He stared at her with obvious frustration and torment. 'Genevieve, *agape*...'

'Don't. Don't stand there and even suggest that you love me,' she begged. 'I thought you did. I really did. But love isn't this. Love isn't measured and it's not conditional, it's not something you can box away. It's not giving someone financial comfort but never giving them yourself.' He flinched, and she knew why, because she truly *understood* him. Perhaps Isabella had said something similar in one of their arguments? Frustration sliced through her. 'If that's all you came to say, you should go.

It's just making an impossible situation even worse, to see you again.'

'You know why I can't offer more.'

'Because you were married, and it was unhappy.'

'Because I made her miserable,' he growled.

'Yes.' She nodded once. 'I know that's what you think. But she stayed with you. She loved you. That was *her* choice—at least you let her make it. You're taking mine away from me.'

'I am making the right choice for both of us.'

'How can you possibly say that?' she shouted. 'How does any part of this feel right?'

'It's how it has to be.'

And it was so obvious from the finality in his tone that he would not change his mind, no matter what she said, that a single tear rolled down her cheek, splashing on her arm.

He dragged her towards him, pulling her close, his hands on her back, as though he was trying to speak with his body, to make her understand something he didn't know how to say. She sobbed, though, and it seemed to pull him out of whatever he was thinking. He stepped backwards, staring at her with an expression that was so much more familiar. The mountain man, rugged, determined and completely in control.

'Would you at least keep this?' he asked, reaching into his pocket and removing the engagement ring. She wrapped her arms around her torso, staring at the stunning teardrop diamond.

'I bought it for you. Your eyes, and the rain that fell the day we met. I saw it and immediately knew it had to be yours. Please keep it—unless you ever need to sell it, then do, of course. Let me at least have that small peace of mind, of knowing that, in some way, I have given you something of value.'

She put her hand out and took the ring; he left before she could tell him he'd given her so much more of value than a diamond. He'd given her the determination and sense of self-worth that had enabled her to reject him, the certainty that she could do more and be more than she'd ever really thought. *That* was what he'd given her, and *that* was what she'd carry, close to her heart.

Nonetheless, as he closed the door behind himself and left her for the last time, she slipped the ring on and stared at it, thinking that it wasn't just like raindrops, but also tears, and that seemed somehow very fitting for how things had ended between them.

One of the first things she discovered, upon returning to Washington, was that Nikos had paid off the hospital debt in its entirety. It was the exact opposite of what she'd asked. He'd ignored her, but she knew why.

He couldn't let himself love her, or be with her, but he felt compelled to care for her. To fix things he could fix. To atone for his perceived sins.

And even though it was something she'd fought, out of pride, she knew how much it would have meant to him to be able to liberate her from James. That doing this must have given him some sense of relief. Of pleasure. And so, she let it rest, at least relieved of the burden of owing James anything. Their connections were, finally, severed.

When first Nikos had come to the island, he had seen it as an emotional torture chamber. A place that was cruel and lonely, that would allow him to torment himself with memories of how much he'd once had before him. He'd relished that idea, exposing himself to the elements, to the threat of animal injury, or heaven knew what else.

The very act of surviving had almost been enough to pull him from his grief, and draw him towards life, and light. It had given him a sense of purpose, to find stone for the cabin, to mix mortar and shape the walls. To turn his back on the trappings of his wealthy life and choose the most haunted and isolated of locations. As he'd triumphed over this landscape, he'd felt a renewed connection to himself, to this world. But still, he'd pushed everyone away. Still he'd known he could never deserve another shot at happiness.

He was right to feel that.

Right to stay true to that commitment. Isabella deserved it.

And what of Genevieve? a voice in his head demanded, so he began to hike across the island, forging a path not taken, always listening for animals, gun at his side, but otherwise stalking with confidence towards the crest of the dormant volcano. Stalking away from thoughts of her. Of what he wanted, and could never have.

At the crest of the mountain, he stopped, and finally allowed himself the weakness of looking towards the mainland, his heart throbbing unbearably at the sight in the distance of what would be Katanos. And wondering if Genevieve was still there, achingly close but for ever out of reach for him. Or was she now in America, without his protection, without him?

Far away, geographically, but for ever a part of him, just as he'd promised?

* * *

It took every ounce of Genevieve's willpower to drag herself to another job interview. It was her sixth this week, and while she thought the others had gone well, all of them had said they'd take a few days to 'think about it'. In the meantime, she hedged her bets. She was conscious of the settlement she'd received from James, and how desperately she wanted to be able to throw it back in his face.

But finding a newspaper who'd take on a journalism major with an almost-four-year career gap wasn't an easy sell, even with the exceptional letters of recommendation she'd secured from the dean of her alma mater.

It wasn't the incessant interviewing that was exhausting her, though.

It was desolation.

Desperation.

Depression.

Loneliness.

She felt, most mornings, as though she'd been rammed by a truck. Her whole body ached, as if she had the worst flu in the world. She slept poorly, barely ate, and couldn't blink without seeing Nikos, exactly as he'd been that first time her eyes had landed on him, stark naked and so heavenly perfect she'd almost wept.

Every minute of every day, she wondered if she'd made a mistake.

If she'd taken him up on his offer, she could at least have known him to be in her life in some capacity. She could have accepted his terms, and known there was at least a chance of seeing him again, of being held by him, made love to by him… Every single part of her ached for him in a way it was difficult to imagine being able to survive.

She'd never known a pain like it. Not with the death of her father, nor her mother, not with James's cruelty and infidelity, certainly not with their divorce. Every single brick in the path of her life had led her to this moment, but she was still so ill-equipped. Because Nikos had left her by choice. Her father and mother had been taken from her, but with no say in the matter. James had been someone she couldn't wait to see the back of.

But with Nikos, she'd offered him everything she had, everything she was, and he'd responded with only the parts of himself he felt safe to share. Money. Financial security.

Never love.

No matter how she looked at it, she came back to the same conclusion, time and time again. Nikos was a man who reached out for what he wanted with both hands. If he'd loved her *enough*, no amount of grief would have stood in his way, no awful past experience with marriage, either. If he'd loved her *enough*, he'd have given her everything he was, and then some, for the rest of their lives.

But he hadn't, and that, therefore, was her answer. She just needed to find a way to forget she loved him—or, at least, to live with the pain of it.

He lost track of the days. They came, and went, came and went. He told Theo not to visit the island. He ignored work. Whatever remnants remained of his life.

And he hoped. He hoped Genevieve was okay. He hoped that if she ever needed him, if her ex-husband ever did anything to hurt her, she would reach out via Theo, knowing he would always support her, when she called.

No matter where she was, no matter when it was. No matter if she was single or married, nothing would change the duty he felt to her, the connection he had to her. The compelling need to protect and serve her, to always be a source of strength in her life, even when he himself couldn't be a part of that life.

Weeks came and went, the weather grew warm, the sun stayed high for longer, showing the shift of seasons, and as it did, his bitterness grew. Worse than he'd ever known it. It enveloped him fully, infusing his body, his bones, his cells, his breath. He could not look out upon this island he'd once loved without seeing Genevieve and thus coming to hate it. Because she wasn't here. She wasn't with him. And that had been his choice.

At the time, he'd fully believed it to be the right decision. He believed he'd done what was right for everyone, including Genevieve. How could he trust himself not to break her, as he'd broken Isabella? How could he trust himself not to be someone else she needed to get over? The thought of hurting her after everything she'd been through…

Except he had hurt her. He'd hurt her by offering so little of himself. He'd hurt her by pushing her away even as he told her he loved her. He'd offered her the whisper of a promise, rather than the all-consuming love she rightfully wanted to hold out for.

Knowing that his need not to hurt her was born of love, he'd thought it was noble. Self-sacrifice in the name of what was right. But the truth was, he was not the same man who'd married Isabella. Looking back, he wouldn't have made that mistake now. He had valued her friendship, and been grateful to her father for the opportunities, and he'd wanted, more than anything, to make her happy. But it hadn't been love in the sense he understood it to be now. Or it had been a childlike version of it, easy to ignore, to focus instead on his work. The mistake hadn't just been neglecting her, it had been taking those vows when they'd meant so much less to him than they had her. He'd been wrong to marry Isabella, wrong not to make her a priority in his life, and he would always regret his actions.

But he was not that man any longer.

Those mistakes had shaped him. From the embers of that regret, out of his guilt and grief, something new had formed, someone different, and it was that person Genevieve had seen and drawn out. It was that person she'd fallen in love with.

As the days came and the days went, a certainty grew inside him that he had made perhaps the worst mistake of his life. He had pushed away a woman who saw him, understood him, knew his imperfections and his whole self, and still wanted him. A woman who was prepared to be patient with him, because she believed he was worth it. He had pushed away the love of his life, after everything she had been willing to offer him—her beautiful, bruised heart.

And suddenly, with a clarity that was both desperate and blinding, he saw that more than anything on this earth, certainly more even than his need for self-flagellation, was his need for Genevieve. Imperfect and terrifying, risks and all, if she was willing to be brave after everything she'd been through, then surely, he could be, too.

CHAPTER FOURTEEN

AFTER FOUR MONTHS, she stopped counting his absence in days. Not because she didn't feel each day stretching like a chasm of grief, but because it was a step towards acceptance. And acceptance, surely, was vital.

Accepting that it really was over.

That she'd been strong enough to walk away from a situation that wasn't right for her. Even when so much of it had been perfectly right—sublimely, utterly, indescribably right—it had been missing the one part she considered non-negotiable. Love. Real, freely given, unconditional, no-holds-barred love.

There was no way she could be with another man who didn't love her as she knew she deserved.

But every day—every single day—she felt that ache of regret when she thought of him. It took all of her energy to get through her workday—as a junior reporter for a respected national paper—without giving away to colleagues her deep, abiding heartbreak. In the same way she'd worn a mask during her marriage, holding it together when she felt miserable inside, she was now playing a part. Going through the motions and hoping no one would notice that she'd left her heart and soul in Greece, and knew she'd never be able to retrieve either.

It was exhausting. Draining, demoralising and completely sapping, so that every day, when she came home to her tiny apartment, she only had enough energy to make a piece of toast, shower and change into pyjamas, before going to bed. She slept fitfully, at best, despite the exhaustion, and woke every morning with a start, as if unable to believe the reality she'd found herself in.

She missed Nikos as a fish would miss water. She missed him with all of herself, and it didn't seem as though it would ever get better. She just had to learn to walk alongside her grief, or it would eat her alive.

The one concession she allowed herself was to continue wearing the engagement ring. Everyone believed her to be engaged to the reclusive billionaire—it would have raised more questions than not, if she'd suddenly stopped wearing it. And having heard the thought he'd put into buying it for her, how could she not? It was a talisman that connected her to him, and she found her eyes drifting to it often as she remembered fractured details of their time together, so her breath would gasp from her on a fresh wave of longing and need.

Of desperate, all-consuming desolation.

It was wrenching. The worst of times.

But she continued to work, knowing that she needed that. She deserved it. Having put her promising career prospects on hold to become the perfect political wife James had wanted, she knew that doing well in her role was a part of reclaiming the person she'd once been. It had mattered deeply to her once, she knew it would again.

Generally, she stayed away from covering political stories. There was too much of a threat of overlap with James, and, despite the true sense of liberation she now felt from that man, she had no interest in stirring up the hornets' nest anew. Her editor had agreed that the potential conflict of interest made it wise for her to stick to other stories.

And yet, on a warm Friday evening, just as she'd walked in the door, her phone started to ring and she saw a colleague's name come up on screen. She contemplated ignoring it, but a phone call out of hours was odd, and Genevieve's curiosity got the better of her.

'Genevieve,' she said, phone tucked under her ear as she hung up her handbag.

'Gen, hey, it's Gary.' Genevieve felt a particular disdain for people who shortened her name when they barely knew her, but she couldn't raise even a hint of that then. She was too tired. Too utterly exhausted. She flopped on the couch. 'I need to call in a favour.'

She arched a brow, wracking her brain for why Gary would think he was owed a favour by her. 'Yeah?'

'This event tonight, I can't cover it. Something's come up. Don't suppose you'd go for me? It's simple. The president will make a speech, a couple of VIPs will talk. You just need to go, get a couple of quotes, an impression of the room, that kind of thing. You up for it?'

No, she wanted to scream. She wasn't up for anything. She wanted to curl up into a ball and cry until she had no tears left. But brittle determination had her nodding. Covering anything presidential was a coup, particularly for a junior journalist. 'Yeah,' she said after a beat. 'I can do that. Text me the details. Will my credentials do?'

'I'll have Tiffany make sure your name is given to the event. You'll be fine.'

'Okay,' she exhaled. 'Good.'

Genevieve had been at events with the president a handful of times, while married to James, so she wasn't as intimidated as she might otherwise have been. She also had the added advantage of knowing how to dress, and do her hair, to look as though she belonged. This, though, was attending in a professional capacity, so, rather than a cocktail dress, she opted for more of a corporate navy trouser suit with a silky oyster camisole underneath. She teamed it with a string of her mother's pearls, and styled her hair in a high ponytail. She hated heels but they were part and parcel of this sort of thing, so she slipped her feet into a pair before regarding herself in the full-length mirror.

Make-up.

She looked like a zombie. Working quickly, she dabbed concealer beneath her eyes, a little bronzer to her cheeks and gloss to her lips, so the next time she checked the mirror, she seemed passably human. Not like someone who'd spent the last four months wishing the world would open up and swallow them whole.

The event was in a five-star hotel on the other side of the city, and, in the interest of living well within her means, she took the bus. Even allowing for public-transport delays, she made it with a couple of minutes to spare.

Something she was not remotely grateful for when the first person she ran into, upon entering the decadent ballroom, was her ex-husband, and his date.

'Well, well,' he drawled, lips flickering with undisguised distaste as he pulled the woman at his side closer. She was very beautiful, in the way all James's mistresses had been, and wore clothes she knew to be to James's taste.

A sense of pity squeezed Genevieve's heart, and she fought an instinct to tell the other woman to run a thousand miles in the opposite direction.

'Senator,' she said, voice clipped, before stepping around him, to leave.

'How's the fiancé?' he asked after her, and her eyes squeezed shut on a wave of fresh pain. Desperate, aching pain. Nikos. The man she thought of as hers, who never really had been.

She turned around though, and forced a smile. 'Fine. I'm sure he'd want me to say hello. He really did enjoy that little chat you both had,' she added.

James's eyes narrowed and she knew that had it not been for the threat of Nikos hanging over his head, he might have said something horrible. Threatened her in some way. Instead, he stood there silently, face turning a shade of puce.

'Aren't you going to ask me how I am, James?' she prompted, anger stirring inside her at how this man had belittled her, all their marriage.

'I don't particularly care.'

'You never did,' she said, with a shrug of her shoulders. 'And I spent so long wondering what I'd done wrong, to make you so cold, and uncaring. But now I see you for what you are: a psychopath.'

He looked as though he wanted to slap something.

'I truly have no idea what I ever saw in you.' She dragged her gaze over his body, and she couldn't help thinking of all the ways in which he didn't match up to Nikos—and never could.

'Have a nice night,' she aimed at his date, before turning and moving swiftly into the crowd, to the area cordoned off for the press. She recognised a couple of journalists she knew, and settled herself amongst them, already enervated by the need for small talk.

It didn't last long. With the precision of a Swiss clock, the president arrived as scheduled, the crowd falling silent with respect. He began to speak of his hopes for a piece of upcoming legislation around childhood hunger, and then began to speak about the government's charity partners, operations that were working in the field, donors to the cause.

'In particular, I would like to thank, as I welcome to the stage, one of the biggest patrons in this space, a personal friend of mine, Nikos Konstantinou.'

Genevieve dropped her phone to the tiled floor, and felt her journalist colleagues' eyes turn to her. Fortunately, the applause somewhat muted the sound as Nikos's name was mentioned. It was little wonder his appearance had caused such a stir: he was famously reclusive. To have him appearing at an event with the president was a huge coup.

Her pulse exploded. Her heart went crazy. Her eyes stung. She knew her face must be a blotchy mess of pale and pink, she could feel the heat and clamminess growing on her, and it only got worse as Nikos, *her Nikos*, strode on stage, more charismatic than any man had ever been, and stood behind the lectern, though his size dwarfed the thing.

'Here,' someone beside her said, passing the phone to her numb fingers. She stuffed it in her pocket without responding. She couldn't. Every single part of her was focused on Nikos as he began to speak, in his beautiful, accented English, his eyes sweeping the crowd and somehow not landing on her. Not seeing her.

And why would he think to look for her? He didn't know what she was doing for work, nor that she'd be there. Which meant he'd come to Washington and not reached out to her. He'd come to the city he knew she lived in, and made no attempt at contact.

'Oh my God,' she whispered, closing her eyes on a wave of renewed pain.

All this time, she'd been pining for him, craving him, missing him with all her soul, and he'd been getting on with his life. Having paid off her debts, he'd clearly absolved himself of any thoughts of her.

She took a step backwards.

'Hey,' a woman snapped with annoyance.

'Sorry,' Genevieve murmured, holding up a hand. But she needed to get out of there. 'I think I'm going to be sick,' she fibbed, figuring there was no better way to clear a cordoned-off space than that. Sure enough, despite the density of journalists, a path formed for her, so she kept her head down and moved quickly towards the edge, and then along the back wall of the room, head down, towards the doors of the venue.

Her heart was racing as she broke out into the warm evening air, her skin flushed, her insides twisting.

But her feet refused to take her further. Her legs were shaking; her breath was hurting. She looked around, in frantic need of a seat, and instead settled on one of the elegant pillars, to lean against. She pressed her back to the cool stone, and closed her eyes, as she tried to process what the heck had just happened. And how she could ever, ever forgive him for this.

* * *

Nikos had seen her the moment he'd walked on stage, and it had taken every single piece of his willpower not to cut through the crowd then and there and pull her into his arms. But though he'd come to the States to see Genevieve, this was a presidential event, and he had no intention of being disrespectful to his friend and the holder of that office.

So he'd begun to speak about the cause, his donations to the charity, keeping his remarks as brief as he possibly could, all the while wondering what she was thinking, how she was, if she was looking at him and missing him as he was her.

He had no way of knowing.

Theo had been able to source minimal information on Genevieve, since her leaving Greece. He knew only where she worked.

Coming here like this had been a gamble, but one he'd had to take. Knowing how he felt about her, he couldn't possibly let another day go by without telling her. Without being brave, as she was brave.

But the sight of her hastily leaving the venue had his whole body on alert. He finished his speech quickly, and slipped off the stage while the crowd was still filling the room with near-deafening applause.

'Genevieve.'

She blinked her eyes open in anguished shock at the voice that had been tormenting her dreams, and her every waking thought, for months on end. She lifted a shaking hand to her mouth, covering the gasp, the sound of shock, of pained betrayal.

It was too much.

She had wanted to see him so badly, but having it take place like this, as a matter of happenstance, because of some charity he was involved with, cut her to the bone.

'Excuse me,' she said, eyes filling with tears as she turned and tried to make her shaking legs cooperate.

But he was right behind her. 'Wait,' he said, and when she didn't stop, his hand reached out and caught hers. 'Please, *agape*. Give me a moment.'

Her heart ached. *Agape*. Love.

'Don't,' she whispered, closing her eyes again as a tear rolled down her cheek. His touch was perfection, but it was also a cruel taunt. She pulled her hand free, and rubbed it against her thigh.

'A moment,' he said, moving to stand in front of her, his eyes raking her face with a look of deep concern. 'I am begging you, Genevieve.'

She tried to swallow, but her throat felt completely constricted, her mouth dry, her brain hardly able to keep up.

'What do you want, Nikos?'

A muscle jerked in his cheek. 'That's difficult to explain.'

Her heart tightened. It shouldn't have been. If it was good news, it would have been the easiest thing in the world to say. *You.*

'Can we speak in private?'

She looked around, for the first time becoming aware that the entrance to the hotel was far from discreet. High-profile guests milled, journalists too.

'I really can't,' she said, shaking her head. 'I mean, I can't talk to you. I can't do this again. It's been four months of torture, of agony, of hoping that each day I would wake up and not feel as though I'd lost a part of myself, and it's not getting better. It's never getting better,' she sobbed, taking a step back from him and twisting her engagement ring out of habit. His eyes dropped to her hand, eyes flaring, and she felt the betraying nature of that gesture, and wanted to curse. 'But seeing you again, it's just going to make it harder. I can't… I can't start all over again. I have to believe I'm making progress, even though it doesn't feel like it. I have to believe that day by day I'm one step closer to getting over you,' she pleaded, as though he could click his fingers and make this all better for her.

Though she'd refused to go somewhere more intimate, Nikos moved his bulky frame to stand between her and the entrance of the hotel, effectively creating privacy for Genevieve by shielding her from view.

'I have to go,' she whispered, shaking her head, staring up at him imploringly. The fact he was here in Washington, and she had no idea for how long, or where he was staying, or any of those vital details, just drove home to her how estranged they now were. Her heart was bursting into a billion pieces.

'Do you think I have not also missed you?' he said, voice dark, as his eyes roamed her face. He was close enough that she could feel his warmth, and her whole body was aching with a need to lean forward and feel his strength, too.

Anger shifted through her chest. 'What?'

'I have been on the island, and you are everywhere there. You are in the trees, the sunlight, the sound of rain on the roof, the fireplace, the bed, you are in my soul, my heart, my very being. I have missed you, Genevieve, in ways I cannot even fathom. I have felt as though I am barely alive, walking this earth, having lost my true north, my reason for being.'

His words were everything she'd wanted to hear, but it was too late. She was so bruised and battered, she couldn't forgive him for putting her through this. She'd given him her heart, and, vitally, her trust, and he'd wanted neither.

'You came to Washington and happened to run into me, and now you're telling me this? What if I hadn't been here tonight? What if I hadn't—?'

'I came here for you,' he contradicted. '*This*—' he gestured to the hotel '—was a guaranteed way of seeing you. I didn't know, otherwise, if you would agree to meet.'

Her jaw dropped. 'But I'm not even meant to be here.'

'I put in a call.'

'You put in a call,' she repeated, dumbfounded.

'I know the owner of your paper.'

She shook her head, her brain not following. 'How do you know where I work?'

A muscle spasmed in his jaw. 'Your stories go online,' he said, and she nodded, because of course they did, and they ran with her byline. A simple Internet search would have shown her pieces.

'You're very talented.' She ignored the pride in his voice, the warmth she might have felt under different circumstances, and focused on what he was saying.

'So you got me to come to a thing that my ex-husband would be at, just so you wouldn't have to face the possibility of rejection?'

His jaw tightened. 'You saw him?'

'Yes, I saw him.'

'And?'

'And what? I told him what a jackass he is, how lucky I am to be free of him.'

The admiration in his expression was unmistakable. And damn it, her heart thwomped in response, warmth spreading through her that she definitely didn't want to feel. 'But you didn't know that,' she snapped.

'Know that you are capable and brave, and more than a match for that weak-minded fool? Do you think I doubted that, *agape*? Do you think any part of me believes you are not able to handle anything life throws at you?'

Her lips parted. The sweetness of that spread through her and then burst into her belly, like fireworks.

She glanced sideways, needing a second to gather her thoughts, because being face to face with Nikos was making it impossible to think straight. She was unbearably torn between what she wanted and what she needed to do, between heart and head, hope and hurt.

'It's been four months,' she whispered, lifting a hand to tuck an errant wisp of hair behind her ear at the same time he went to do the same, so their fingers brushed and her eyes flew back to his face, her heart leaping into her throat. 'Four months,' she said, imploringly, staring at him, as his fingers curled around hers and then laced through them, lifting them to his lips and pressing a kiss to her knuckles.

'Yes, it's been the worst four months of my life,' he said, eyes hooked to hers. 'Like you, I kept thinking I would get past it, that I would wake up one day and feel like myself again, but I cannot. I will never get used to missing you, my darling, my love.'

She shook her head, willing herself not to believe it.

'I was so afraid of hurting you. After Isabella, how

could I trust that I would do what was right by you? Even knowing my heart belonged to you, I could never ask you to trust me with it, to trust me with your life.'

'That's my decision to make.'

'Yes, it always was,' he agreed. 'And you made it. You gave yourself to me, and instead of taking that gift with both hands open, I fled, because even the remotest possibility of hurting you, of making you miserable, of being someone else you had to get over, as you have James… I ran from that, Genevieve.'

She closed her eyes. 'You hurt me, anyway.'

'I hurt us both.'

She bit back a sob at the truth of that.

'I came to Washington because I needed to tell you that I was wrong.'

She kept her eyes closed. His hand squeezed hers.

'I will never forgive myself for how I was with Isabella, but I'm not that man any more, and you are not her. We are different; everything about us is. With my dying breath, I will honour and cherish you, if you will let me. Without me realising it, you have become the most important thing in my life, the only thing I seem to care about, these days. All I ask is that you consider letting me back in, to prove to you that I deserve what you so freely offered, in Katanos.'

She couldn't bite back this sob. It burst from her as she opened her eyes and stared at him imploringly.

'What does that mean?' she finally whispered.

'That I want to date you,' he said. 'That I want to cherish and adore you, to stand by your side as you make your journalistic mark on the world, supporting your work, your goals, being whatever you need me to be, until you realise that your first instinct about us was right. We are meant to be together, and I will be here, if you'll let me, every single day, until you see that what we share is unique and wonderful—and truly meant to be.'

A tear slid down her cheek. 'And if I *won't* let you?' she whispered, hauntingly.

Grief passed over his features, but he rallied quickly. 'Then I'll still be here, just in case you change your mind. If you need me, or want me, or just need a friend to talk to about your day.' He squeezed her hand again. 'In whatever capacity you'll have me, I'm here. I love you, Genevieve, but I'm not stupid enough to expect this to be easy. I recognise what it took for you to admit your feelings for me, to even *feel* them at all. And I know what my reaction must have done to you. I am for ever sorry for that.'

Another tear slid down her cheek and this time, he lifted his spare hand to dab it away.

'Can we start with you giving me your number?' he asked, and her heart lurched, because it was such a tender, gentle, uncertain request, so utterly nothing compared to what Genevieve wanted, but a part of her felt the need to cling to her protective barriers, just a while longer. Even knowing that he could obtain her number easily, through one of his contacts, she appreciated that he was *asking* her. Respecting her autonomy.

'Yes,' she said, nodding slowly. 'I'll give you my number.'

He expelled a slow breath of relief. 'And I'll be sure to use it.'

CHAPTER FIFTEEN

IT WASN'T EVEN half an hour later when his text came through.

Are you free for dinner tomorrow?

Her heart stampeded through her body, fairly trampling her other organs, and she couldn't stop smiling as she wrote her reply:

Depends. Where would we go?

He named a renowned Greek restaurant, and she closed her eyes on a wave of memories of dinners in Athens as she tapped out a reply.

Well, a girl does have to eat.

His reply was instant.

I'll pick you up at eight.

Eight o'clock! How on earth was she meant to wait that

long? Particularly given she'd been falling asleep well before that, these past few months.

But there was something about having seen Nikos again, and having the prospect of a date with him on the horizon, that made her whole body hum and buzz with energy all day.

By six o'clock, she was tempted to text him and ask him to come over earlier. She didn't, though. She stuck to their original plan, and she took her time getting ready. A long soak in the tub, shaved legs, body moisturised all over, make-up carefully applied to be dewy and minimalistic, hair loose and brushed until it shone, and an outfit chosen with care.

She was determined to keep him at arm's length, but that didn't mean she didn't want to also drive him a little crazy. She was pretty sure he knew what he'd been missing, and would do anything to go back in time and change the way things had gone, on the yacht. Nonetheless, a little reminder would do him the world of good.

She chose a silky slip dress, emerald green in colour, and teamed it with a strappy pair of heels and a matching clutch. The dress was cut on the bias and fell to a couple of inches above the knees, showing her tanned legs and just enough of a hint of cleavage.

When he rang her doorbell, she took a moment to apply a deep red lipstick before pulling the door inwards.

His deep-throated curse was enough to make her body sing.

'Ready?' she asked, blinking sweetly, all too aware of the effect she was having on him.

To be fair, though he'd probably spent considerably less time on his appearance, she was no less breathless and hot under the proverbial collar at the sight of him in a suit, custom shoes, with his hair brushed back from his brow. The thing with Nikos was that no matter what he wore, that ruthless, powerful animalism was just beneath the surface, waiting to burst out. From nowhere, she imagined him pushing her into the apartment and taking her against the wall, hard and fast, until she was crying his name, and warm heat pooled between her legs.

'My car is downstairs,' he said, and her eyes widened as she remembered the time they'd made love in his car.

Suddenly, the idea of keeping him at any kind of distance seemed ridiculous. She believed that he loved her. She knew he did. And she also knew he was sorry. Whatever evidence she'd been hoping to attain to allow her to trust him again seemed completely unnecessary. When she looked back on her time with this man, she saw a thousand ways he'd shown himself to be trustworthy and decent, honourable and kind.

'Let's go to dinner,' she said, against every single wish and instinct she possessed.

As she closed the door to her apartment behind herself, he put a hand in the small of her back, holding her against his side.

To her surprise, he'd booked out the entire restaurant, and their table was in an alcove away from the windows, meaning there was no intrusion into their privacy. She didn't want to think about what it would have cost to secure a venue like this at the last minute. All she could think about was what it meant. No part of this was to do with their original plan, to put James in his place, and get him off her back.

This was about Nikos and Genevieve, and the love they shared.

'Do you think it's weird,' she asked, after dinner, when they were back in his car, on the way to her apartment, 'that I still wear your ring?'

His eyes held hers and then he reached for her hand and touched the diamond. 'On the contrary, it is right, and perfect. My deepest wish is that you will continue to wear it, all the way until such time I can add another ring to be its pair.'

Her heart turned over in her chest and her lips parted.

He swore softly then. 'I don't mean to rush you. I don't mean—it is obviously my wish, but there is plenty of time, my darling, for the rest of our lives.'

She turned away from him rather than answering, because her smile made it impossible to speak.

At her door, he kissed her goodnight on the cheek and then turned to leave. He couldn't push this too hard. He knew it would take time for Genevieve to feel safe trusting him again, to know that he was worthy of all the love and faith she'd put in him before. But hell, he'd wanted to go inside with her more than he could say. Not just because his body was yearning for hers in a way he could hardly live with, but also because he couldn't get enough of her.

Listening to her talk about her work, and how proud she was, how obviously good she was. Listening to her talk about anything, hearing her laugh and knowing he'd caused it. He just wanted to breathe the same air as her, for as long as he could.

For now, though, just the whisper of hope she'd given him had to be enough.

* * *

Dinner tonight? The text came through the following morning, and her heart lurched in response.

She had barely slept, but this time, her wakefulness had been caused by the most delirious happiness. Genevieve had lain awake in bed and replayed every moment, every touch, every look, until her heart was humming and her insides were twisting.

She tapped out a reply: Why don't I cook?

I don't want to put you to the trouble.

Nonsense. You cooked for me on the island. It seems only fair.

There was a lengthy pause before he responded: What can I bring?

He arrived with a bottle of wine and the biggest bunch of flowers she'd ever seen. Genevieve buried her face in the blooms to stop from launching into his arms and kissing him with all her passion and love. She arranged them in a vase while he uncorked the wine and poured two glasses.

She had thought she might feel ashamed of her apartment. She knew it was small, in a rough neighbourhood, and pretty cheaply furnished, but instead, when he looked around and had that same proud expression on his face, she just felt alive. Adored. Appreciated, for how hard she was working to achieve her financial freedom. Because she knew he saw that, he would never think she wasn't someone who wanted to stand on her own two feet.

His money was so irrelevant to what they were. It

barely even entered her mind to consider the disparity between them, despite his generosity with the hospital bills.

Genevieve had learned to cook from a young age, and she was very good at it. She made creamy garlic prawns for entrée, and then lamb for main course, as he had served them in Greece, and he ate it appreciatively, marvelling at how skilled she was in the kitchen, until she laughed and told him he really needed to stop.

His eyes lifted to hers, and the smile in the creases of his face shifted, sobering. 'I can't stop,' he said, shaking his head. 'I told myself I wouldn't rush this, but being here with you, in your apartment, there is a part of me that wants, more than anything, to press fast forward and start the rest of our lives now.' He closed his eyes then. 'I know it's selfish of me. It's just…for a brief time, I got to call you my fiancée, to know that you were, at least to the rest of the world, truly mine. I cannot wait for a time I can do that again.'

Her heart turned over in her chest and every single piece of her seemed to click in together. She felt the sting of tears in the back of her throat as she took a quick gulp of wine.

'Well,' she said, a little unevenly. 'We never technically announced that our engagement was at an end.'

He stared at her without reacting, but because she knew him, she understood what that took for him to do.

'I suppose it wouldn't hurt for you to still refer to me as your fiancée.'

He nodded slowly. 'Because of James?'

She blanched, and stood then, coming around to the

other side of the table and manoeuvring herself into his lap. 'No, not at all. This would be just for you and me.'

'Are you saying—would this be real?'

Her eyes sparkled with unshed tears as she nodded. 'I think that's a great idea.'

She couldn't say who kissed whom first, but their lips connected and it was as though every star in the heavens went supernova simultaneously. Lights flashed in her eyes and her body rejoiced, as did her heart, at the certainty that she was with the man she was destined to find.

And the more she thought about it, the more she truly felt that destiny had had a hand in their meeting. The storm that had blown up out of nowhere, her hiring a sailboat just to feel close to her father—she could never shake the sense that perhaps it had been her parents, and Isabella, who'd somehow created the magic that had brought Genevieve to Nikos in the most unlikely of circumstances.

One week after dinner in Genevieve's apartment, they were at Nikos's luxurious Washington home, and without her realising at first what he was doing, Nikos was down on one knee, holding out another black velvet box.

Her heart stammered in her chest as she shook her head.

'I never got a chance to propose properly,' he said, clasping her hands. 'And I want to.'

'It was proper enough,' she said, because that night remained in her memory as one of the happiest of her life.

'Not for you, my darling. For you I would do anything, go anywhere. I kneel before you as a man who has fallen completely in love, with all of my being. You are the beginning and end of my days, the entirety of my hopes.

A thousand lifetimes with you could never be enough. Please, say you'll marry me, because you know that I love you and will always honour you, because you understand that, from this day on, my life will be spent in the service of you and yours.'

She nodded, tears streaming. 'Of course, Nikos, of course. But my ring—'

He cracked open the box to reveal teardrop diamond earrings, the same glorious shade of blue.

'I had them made, to match,' he said. 'I could not get you out of my head, and I knew you should have them. Even if you chose to sell them.'

She gasped. 'I would never.'

'Good.' He stood, inspecting her ears before removing one from the box and beginning to insert it. 'Will you wear them, Genevieve, my darling, and know that they are the beginning of the expression of my love for you, a love that will guide me for all time?'

She could barely cope with the sincerity and extremeness of his sentiment; yet she understood it, because she felt the same.

She waited until he had both earrings in place before she answered, by pressing a hand to his chest to put a little distance between them.

'How about,' she said, reaching behind her back and feeling for her zip, 'I wear them—' she began to ease it down '—and absolutely nothing else, for the rest of the night?'

She saw his Adam's apple move as he stared across at her.

'And your ring?'

She stripped out of her underwear, until she wore only a pair of heels, her earrings and diamond ring.

His eyes fell to it and she smiled. 'Oh, I'm never, ever taking that off.'

EPILOGUE

LITTLE BY LITTLE, with Genevieve's help, Nikos began to fully let go of his demons. While he'd already come to understand how changed he was, by life and circumstances, he also finally accepted that he had been blaming himself too harshly for his marriage. Isabella had hated his work hours, but she *had* been happy. He finally let himself hear that, from her father, her friends. People that had once been in his life, he'd spent years pushing away, he now got to know again. And in hearing them speak of Isabella, he realised that Genevieve had been right about that, too. His late wife deserved better than to have become a pain point in his life.

Working with Isabella's father, Nikos and Genevieve set up a charity in Isabella's name. Far from ever expressing even a hint of jealousy, Genevieve supported Nikos tirelessly in this work, because she understood how far he'd come. How healthy it was for him to honour Isabella, as a mark of his progress. He no longer had his head in the sand, and that was because of Genevieve.

As Genevieve built her career, he supported her, understanding her drive to succeed, the way she'd been held back by James. No doubt the egotistical man had been jealous of her obvious talent.

Nikos was not completely true to his word, however. He couldn't resist stymying the other man's career. A few well-placed calls ensured he received a challenge at the next election; he lost his senatorial seat, and left Washington, to live a life of quiet, yet wealthy, obscurity.

Genevieve didn't care, though. James had long ago lost any power to hurt her. He was just a speed bump in her life, a brief chapter that had served one wonderful purpose: to bring her to Nikos.

They waited to have children. While they both knew they wanted a family, Genevieve's career was going from strength to strength, and Nikos knew the timing decision had to be hers.

They were blessed with three girls, and each of them was raised to be strong and independent, to know their worth and use their voice powerfully. Isabella, and her father, were a part of their lives, always. They spoke of Isabella as someone Nikos loved, and they included her father in all family events, so that he became a grandfather to their children, a valued member of their family.

* * * * *